What's wrong with

M.E.N.

C.W. BURNETT

What's wrong with

M.E.N.

C.W. BURNETT

All I Do Is Pen Publishing LLC.
1603 Capitol Ave. Ste. #310
Cheyenne, Wy 82001
www.allidoispen.com

First printing: 2019

Cover design by: Benedicta Buatsie

Graphic design and layout by: Hub Design

Edited by: Before You Publish LLC.

ISBN: 9781700950345

To my beautiful Summer De'Che,

Daddy loves you more than anything on God's green Earth

Thank you for being the motivation behind everything I do

Acknowledgements

I would like to thank God for giving me the focus and ability to complete this novel; my daughter, Summer Burnett for giving me the motivation to turn my life around; my sister, Mia Campbell for always being my rock and voice of reason; my mother, Lynnette Robinson for always being in my corner regardless of the circumstance; my grandmother, Linda Meredith for all of her prayers. I would also like to thank my friend and graphic designer, Jae Noirel for treating this project as if it was his own; my cousins, Chaz Sonnirea and Johnathan Green for all of the wisdom they shared during a dark time in my life; my good friends Ken Collins, Terran Smith, Derron Wiggins, Deon Williams, Giorgio McKinney, Brandon Pettiway and to all my family for the love and support.

CHAPTER ONE

It was a beautiful Sunday evening in Los Angeles. The ladies couldn't have chosen a better night to celebrate. Eve's divorce became final earlier in the week, and a night out with the girls would serve as the icing on the cake.

The crew decided to fall into a popular lounge located in West Hollywood called, "The Spot." This venue was known for bringing out Hollywood's A-list celebrities, as well as big-named athletes. Flashing lights, hookah fumes, and confetti blazed the building as waitresses carried out elaborate dance routines with sparklers and bottles in each hand. Typically, Monique, Eve, and Na'Tosha would've preferred something more low-key. But the opportunity to watch Grammy Award winning artist, H.E.R. perform was too tempting to turn down.

Eve had been in contact with one of the lounge's promoters throughout the month. The thought of not being V.I.P. hadn't even crossed her mind. This night was too important to be crammed amongst the general population.

The promoter met the ladies at the door. After a few words, he checked Eve's name off the list and directed the crew towards their designated area. "Your section is in the corner to the left. A waitress will be over shortly to take your drink orders and to put your card on file for bottle service. I'm pretty busy, as you can see, but I'll try my best to check on y'all in a few."

As the three approached the section, they couldn't help but notice that it was already occupied. A group of six flashy-looking guys and four skimpy-dressed women were comfortably nestled on the soft, tan leather couches reserved for Eve. Someone had even used the sign with her name on it as a coaster.

Eve politely summoned the attention of one of the guys seated in her assigned area. "Excuse me, sir... But, umm... I think you all have the wrong section. We actually reserved this spot a couple weeks ago."

The slim, heavily tattooed guy glanced over at Eve. He stared at her momentarily before rudely continuing his conversation with one of the erotically attired females seated beside him. Eve's kind, soft spoken approach obviously hadn't worked on him. It was apparent that a little more emphasis would be required.

Monique decided that she'd give it a try. She cleared her throat and tapped one of his buddies on the arm. "Hey, obviously there's been a mistake. This section belongs to us... Now we'd appreciate if you'd—" Monique was interrupted by a dark, large bearded man.

The oversized, beast of a man took a swig from his gigantic champagne bottle. "Baby, I'm sorry to tell you but this us right here... And we ain't goin' nowhere." His massive neck supported several gold chains, and many colors illuminated from the iced out Patek Philippe watch he was wearing on his wrist. The guy had football player written all over him. "Tell you what, tho'... If yo' fine-ass potna in the red come sit on my lap, y'all can turn up wit' us." He nodded in Na'Tosha's direction.

Na'Tosha was wearing a tightly fitted, maxi dress. To say that it perfectly hugged her heavenly, curvaceous body would be an understatement. Na'Tosha's coke bottle figure could easily make a grown man cry. The shade of red that she wore complemented her honey-brown complexion to a T. She accessorized the ensemble with matte red lipstick, diamond looped earrings, and a gold choker. A Chanel clutch purse and a pair of red bottoms put the cherry on top. The other two ladies in the crew were baddies in their own right, however, it was Na'Tosha who turned heads everywhere that she went. The unwanted attention from big monster man wasn't anything new. Now, what came out next from the mouth of his yellow-teethed, bumpy-faced, bug-eyed, nappy-headed, tight-clothes wearing protégé was what almost set off a riot.

"Fareal tho', big homie... That thick-ass bitch can get the dick right now."

The three women snapped their heads around so fast that they almost caught whiplash.

Na'Tosha was enraged by the disrespect, thinking he obviously didn't realize that he was messing with the wrong one. She started taking off her shoes and earrings. It was time to give the punk a lesson in manners. "Lemme tell you something you whack, lame, fake jewelry wearin', bitch-ass nigga."

All the guys in the section stared in Na'Tosha's direction. A few of them shamefully examined their own jewelry, indicating that it might've been some truth behind her bold observation.

Eve attempted to calm Na'Tosha down by pulling her away. "Whoa. Chill, Na'Tosha. You know these dudes not playing fair nowadays."

"Hell nah, fuck that. I'm tired of these fake niggas thinkin' they can play us however they want, whenever they feel."

Monique stepped closer towards the men, voicing what initially appeared to be a sincere change of heart, "You know what? It's okay, fellas. We don't want any problems. Come on y'all, we can just sit at the bar. Enjoy your section—Bums." Monique reached over and snatched a drink from a waitress's tray. In one motion, she threw it in the face of the young ugly guy with the foul mouth. Then, she flipped the bird to the entire crew and switched her hips in route to the bar with the other two ladies following closely behind.

The ugly guy held his face in agony as tequila burned his crusty, yellow eyes. A couple of his boys yelled out expletives towards the ladies as the three scurried off. While a few others in the group laughed, knowing that 'crater face' actually got what he deserved.

The ladies were now seated at the bar, holding drinks.

"I swear, niggas ain't shit," Na'Tosha expressed.

"Ain't none of 'em worth a damn," said Monique.

"Bitch, I thought you wasn't cussin' no more?" Na'Tosha turned to Monique.

"Damn isn't a curse word. And if it is... Welp. Then, fuck it." Monique sipped from her drink and shrugged her shoulders and added, "Oops."

Eve placed a hand under her chin and looked down at the counter. It was obvious something was on her mind. She slowly stirred her drink before uttering, "Hey, y'all... Am I wrong for feeling like there are still some good men out there? Somewhere?"

"Barely," said Monique in a playful, high-pitched voice.

"Of course, Eve. There are still plenty of good men out there." Na'Tosha's tone dripped with sarcasm.

"See, even Na'Tosha knows good men still exist." Eve exhaled.

"Yeah, I do know... Just so happen that they all on the down low suckin' dii—"

Eve interrupted, "—Okay sooo... Ladies, it's been a while since we've gotten together, right?"

Na'Tosha clapped her hands. "Yaaaass, bitch, yaaaasss. Congratulations, boo."

Eve waved her hands in the air. "Thank you."

Monique raised her glass for a toast. "I know that it's been rough, but we are so happy for the start of your new journey."

"Yes, girl... I'm so over all the back and forth with the lawyers, judges, and having to relive the bullshit from the past."

Monique gently rubbed Eve's back. "Don't worry. Divorces take time to move on from. Soon it'll all be a distant memory."

"I know... It's just that he left me with nothing. I gave him ten years, two kids, and put up with all his extra-marital bullshit. And all I have to show for it is a car that always needs work, a dog I can't afford, and a measly six-hundred dollars a month in child support... I just pray that this apartment comes through for me."

Monique scooted closer towards Eve. "Now you know I have plenty of room for you and the kids at my house."

"I know, I know... Thanks, but I wouldn't want to be any more of a burden on you than what I already am. You've done so much as it is... Plus, you know my kids' cray cray. We'd wear out our welcome in a heartbeat."

"Bitch, last time I watched yo' bay-bay kids, they damn near got me put out. D.J. ass was on my Snapchat posting shit like he my man, and lil' Ms. Denisha was all in the video, screaming out 'gang-gang'," said Na'Tosha, before sipping from her drink.

Eve shamefully placed a hand over her face. "Girl, I'm so sorry."

"Umm, why are you apologizing? Excuse me, Ms. Thang. Can you please explain to our apologetic friend exactly what you were doing in the midst of all of this?" asked Monique.

"Bitch, my ratchet ass was right there wit' 'em, twerkin' like BAM BAM BAM BAM." Na'Tosha raised a leg and twerked on Monique's lap.

A random guy stopped and admired her juicy cakes bouncing up and down.

"Ugghh. Boo, nigga," Na'Tosha said, giving him the leftover anger from the thieves in the V.I.P. section.

The unwanted spectator dropped his head and continued on his way.

"You so damn rude," said Monique, while laughing.

"You know I'm a beast on these niggas." Na'Tosha slapped five with Monique.

Monique slipped an arm around Eve's shoulder. "All jokes aside, you know that I'm here if you need me. You, my nephew, and niece are always welcome." Monique sucked through the black straw of her Long Island Iced Tea, causing what was left of it to bubble against the half melted iced cubes. "Girl, I'm so damn lonely, I could use some company right about now."

"Lonely? Weren't you getting lots of dates on that dating app not too long ago?" asked Eve.

Monique took a big gulp from her drink. "Lord Jesus, please don't remind me."

"I mean damn, was it that bad?" Eve turned towards Monique.

"Girl, it was terrible. All three of 'em."

"Bitch, are you gon' tell us what happened, or nah?" asked Na'-Tosha.

"Well, if y'all really want to know... I guess I'll start from the top and work my way down."

DATE #1: Vincent Baker

Monique fanned away smoke as she wandered into the raunchy, dimly lit sports bar to meet her first online date. Plastic cups, beer bottles, and chicken wing bones littered the hardwood surface. Vincent Baker was a union electrician from Inglewood and had definitely fit Monique's physical requirements: tall, dark, and muscularly built. As Monique approached closely, she noticed that Vincent was dressed in what appeared to be construction gear.

Vincent was seated inside of a booth towards the back of the bar. He seemed to be in the midst of a heated phone conversation so Monique took a seat, and patiently waited to make a formal introduction.

After several minutes, Vincent noticed her growing impatience. He dished out a few, last-minute, insults before abruptly ending his call.

Monique, genuinely concerned, simply asked, "Is everything okay?"

Vincent, with a look of frustration, placed his phone inside of his neon green, hazard vest pocket.

"Yeah, my bad about that. It was just my baby momma trippin'... Again."

Monique immediately mentally noted a red flag. At her age, it would be foolish to write off all men with children. However, baby momma drama wasn't something she was willing to get involved with.

"Oh, wow. Okay... Sorry to hear that."

"It's coo'. She just be trippin' on everything I do..." Vincent continued to complain about his child's mother. He rambled on and on about things that weren't meant to be discussed on a first date, or any other date for that matter.

Monique tapped her heel against the dirty floor and cut her eyes every time he tried to make eye contact. As Vincent went deeper into his dysfunctional co-parenting situation, she noticed his voice starting to crack.

"I take care of my kids. Birthdays, doctor's appointments, daddy donut day, all that. I'm there." Vincent tapped his chest proudly. "All she ever wanna do is talk about child support. All right... I ain't gon' lie, I missed a couple payments, but we all fall short sometimes, you feel me?

They laid-off a bunch of people at the plant a while back, and I missed hella' days because Mike-Mike was trippin' at school, and then for Lay-Lay asthma problems. They ended up giving me the boot. I bounced back tho'. I'm working now, that's all that matters."

Vincent's constant babbling, along with his poor vocabulary, left Monique completely disinterested.

She grabbed her coat and purse, before mapping out her escape route.

"Hey, look. I'm sorry but I have to go." Without looking back, Monique power-walked her way towards the exit. Right before she placed her hand onto the door, Vincent yelled out.

"But I didn't even get to finish telling you my story."

DATE#2: Jontay Smith

Monique gave the dating app another shot. She figured that it couldn't get any worse than baby momma drama man. Wow, was she wrong. Monique scheduled a lunch date with online guy number two. It was a gorgeous day and a perfect opportunity to take advantage of the restaurant's patio area. She checked her watch, noticing that her date was late.

Minutes later a brand new, tricked out BMW X6 rolled up blasting loud gangster rap music. A trail of marijuana smoke followed as Jontay exited his pimped-out ride. He grinned excitedly after spotting Monique seated on the terrace. His pants were sagging halfway down his backside. Jontay's Cuban link chain and mouth full of gold teeth reflected sun rays into her eyes.

Monique was attracted to low-key, clean cut guys. So, Jontay's gaudy, rapper-like image wasn't cutting it. She questioned how the two even matched in the first place.

All wasn't lost in regard to Jontay's appearance. He was a solid 6'3" with light brown eyes. His hair was in a neatly tapered afro with curls on top. Monique compared him to a grown up version of LDB from the 90s R&B group, Immature.

Jontay made his way over to Monique's table. "Hey sexy, how are you?"

"Sir, the name is Monique."

"My bad, baby. It's nice to finally meet you."

Monique pointed to her watch. "A little late, aren't we? Oh... And please, don't call me baby. Monique will work just fine."

Jontay flashed his gold-plated smile. "Yeah, my bad about that too... I kind of got caught in traffic," Jontay's phone rang. "Hold on a second, *Hello? Yeah. What's good... Nah, nah he already owe me money, bruh... Still, it don't matter. Tell him until he take care of that last bill, ain't nothin' happenin'... A'ight coo',"* Jontay ended the call. "Sorry about that, boo... Did you have a chance to look at the menu yet?"

Monique was bothered by Jontay's disregard for her name but did her best to remain calm. "I'd really appreciate if you'd cut out the pet names... And to answer your question, yes, I've actually had a chance to glance at the menu. The shrimp and grits sound pretty good. What do you have a taste for?"

Jontay's phone rang again. "Hold up, lil' momma. Give me one more minute. *Hello...Where da' fuck you been at... But you was supposed to drop dat' off last week... Stop lying... No, you didn't... No, you didn't... Tone nem would've been checked you off the list by now... You got till midnight, homie, or it's curtains."*

Mortified, Monique asked, "Hey, is everything okay?"

Jontay took a few seconds and slowly breathed in and out. "Yeah, yeah I'm good."

Monique decided to change the subject. "Sooo, I couldn't help but notice that you're dressed a little differently from your profile picture."

Jontay pondered for a few seconds before smiling. "Oh yeah... You're right. I took that pic right after I left court. You know I had to be suited and booted when them charges got dropped. Wait 'til you see how Imma come thru when I get off probation. Three more months and I'm thru wit' they ass."

Monique buried her head inside of the menu. Jontay's "thug life" behavior was a complete turnoff. She certainly wasn't down to be nobody's trap queen. After excusing herself to the restroom, Monique made a break for the exit. Maybe online dating just wasn't meant for her.

DATE#3: Gerald Thompson

Monique questioned whether or not she'd ever be able to find a good man. It'd been well over a month since her date with "Big Meech Jr." Not to mention, going on a year since the last time she'd gotten some. Monique wasn't interested in a "friends with benefits" situation. Nonetheless, she thought that she would have at least found a potential suitor for the cookie by now. Guess the cookie would just have to remain in the jar for now.

Out of sheer boredom, Monique clicked onto the same dating app that had failed her thus far. She was on a break in between meetings and figured she'd kill a little time by swiping. Monique repeatedly swiped left, rejecting profiles as she'd been so accustomed to doing. No one in particular caught her eye. Until, she stumbled onto the profile of Mr. Gerald Thompson. She was a sucker for an educated, career-driven man with a nice smile, and Gerald matched the criteria.

The two messaged regularly over the next few weeks. During that time, they discovered they had many things in common. Gerald asked Monique out on a date and against her better judgement, she agreed.

Upon arrival, Monique made sure that she was dressed to impress, wearing a blue romper, with a ripped jean jacket that went great with her designer heels. Monique sprayed on her favorite perfume, Marc Jacobs' Decadence. After checking her make-up in the rear-view mirror, Mo was good to go and got out of her car. A host greeted her at the door and escorted her over to where Gerald was already seated. Then, he kindly removed her jacket as Gerald prepared to introduce himself.

"You must be Monique? Hi, I'm Gerald."

"I am her, indeed... Nice to meet you," Monique took a seat and gave Gerald a computer-like body scan. First, she analyzed his haircut, his teeth, and finally, she intentionally dropped her napkin, looked underneath the table, and took a peek at Gary's shoe game. "Excuse me. I'm so sorry... I can be a bit clumsy at times."

Gerald smiled. "Did you get a good look at the shoes while you were down there?"

"Actually, I did take a quick glance." Monique blushed. "And I must say, they're nice."

"Thanks... So, are yours. Jimmy Choo, right?"

Monique was impressed by his accuracy. "Yes, great guess."

"It's only a guess if you're unsure."

Monique smiled. It was something sexy about a man who was self-assured.

The two had an amazing time laughing, joking, playfully debating, and connecting over a wonderful meal. Monique hadn't experienced a date like this in a long time. Gerald was a perfect gentleman. His etiquette was a breath of fresh air compared to what she'd recently come across in the cyber dating world. After sharing a huge slice of triple layered chocolate cake, they both realized it was time to call it a night.

"This was so much fun, Monique... We have to do it again."

"Yes, I agree. I have to be honest though... I was a little worried. I haven't had a lot of success with dating, so I definitely had my doubts."

"That's totally understandable. I've had my fair share of failed dates as well, so I know exactly what you mean. I'm just glad that I was able to meet your expectations."

Monique gazed into Gerald's eyes. "You've definitely done that."

Gerald smiled and flagged down the waitress. He handed the server five crispy one-hundred-dollar bills. "Ma'am, your service has been great. Keep the change."

"Wow. Oh, my God. Thank you, sir. You both have a great evening." The waitress skipped away ecstatically gripping the newly minted, blue-faced currency.

Monique duly noted Gerald's generosity. As they both stood to exit the restaurant, she reached down to grab her purse. She looked back at Gerald and noticed he seemed to be a lot shorter than what she originally thought. In fact, Monique appeared to be almost a foot taller than him. This couldn't be so. His feet didn't appear to dangle when she looked at his Ferragamo loafers. On the other hand, she did only peer momentarily. Her mind had to be playing tricks on her. Monique was 5'6" and slightly under 6' with heels on. Gerald appeared to be at least a few inches taller sitting down, or else she would've definitely noticed.

Gerald leaned in for a hug and the top of his neatly cut fade only came to the cleavage of Monique's breasts. This was certainly a deal breaker. No way would she ever let a small fish swim anywhere near her deep sea. Monique scratched her head.

"Wow... Umm... Is it just me, or did you seem a lot taller sitting down?"

Gerald's confidence remained strong. "It's funny that you mention it. I bring a booster seat when I come to restaurants." He handed Monique the booster. "See... I even have my initials carved in it, so it doesn't get mixed up with all the others. You'd be surprised how many of these places look at me crazy when I walk out with this thing. As if I'd steal a booster seat. Come on now."

Monique was at a loss for words. It was confirmed. No more online dating.

•••

Eve and Na'Tosha looked on with their jaws dropped. Eve was speechless, but of course that wasn't the case for Na'Tosha.

"Damn, bitch that was terrible," shouted Na'Tosha.

"I tried to tell y'all."

"Well, Gerald didn't seem so bad to me. It sounded like y'all had good chemistry," said Eve.

Na'Tosha turned to Eve. "Bitch, was you listening? The man was a midget... Shrimp... Toddler man."

"Don't be so shallow. Nobody's perfect. Sometimes you have to compromise in order to find love."

Na'Tosha rolled her eyes. "Honey, compromising is one thing. But the man brought a damn booster seat with his initials carved in it. Ain't nobody got time for dat."

Eve conceded, "I guess you do have a point there."

"Of course, I got a point. Anyway... New subject... So, Monique, whatever happened to the guy you was talking to a while back? Marcus, right?"

Monique corrected her, "You mean Mario?"

Na'Tosha sucked her teeth. Whateva, heffa. Mario, Marcus all dat' shit sound da' same to me. Yo' ass know exactly who I was talkin' 'bout." Na'Tosha was terrible with names—and at controlling her foul tongue.

"Yeah, whatever happened to Mr. Mario? I thought you liked him?" asked Eve.

"I did kind of like him, but I had to fall back. Something just wasn't checking out."

Eve was surprised by Monique's response. "Hold up... Just wasn't checking out?"

Eve and Na'Tosha tallied up Mario's credentials.

Eve said, "He's tall."

Na'Tosha responded, "Check."

Eve added, "Handsome."

Na'Tosha again responded, "Check."

Eve, "Stable."

Na'Tosha, "Check."

Eve added, "No kids."

Na'Tosha, "Check."

Eve, "Great career."

Na'Tosha ended with, "Big fat check."

Monique shrugged her shoulders and summoned the bartender for another drink.

"I don't know what it is, y'all. I just can't put my finger on it."

"His thang must be small, huh?" asked Na'Tosha.

Eve popped Na'Tosha on the arm. "Un uhh. That's so rude. Don't do that," Eve paused momentarily, cocked her head to the side, and sipped from her straw, "But since she did ask... Is it?"

Monique rolled her eyes. "No, that's not it... Well, at least I hope it isn't... All I can say is, my intuition kept sending me signals. He just seemed too good to be true."

Na'Tosha cosigned, "And when it seems too good to be true, guess what? The shit be too good to be true."

Eve disagreed, "Y'all both are tripping. Let God send me a man with a resumé like that."

"And you ain't gon' do a damn thang wit' it. Hoe, you was tied down too long. You washed up," said Na'Tosha.

"Hold up now... Don't get it twisted, boo boo. This thang is still sweet and gushy. Hello."

Monique high-fived Eve. "I know that's right, girl. You better let her know."

"Yeah, yeah whateva. Speaking of sweet and gushy... When you gon' gush all over that cute lil' coach from D.J. basketball team?" asked Na'Tosha.

Monique chimed in, "Oh, yeah girl, he isss cute."

"See, Eve ass think she slick. We see the way you be looking at him."

"It ain't even like that," said Eve.

Na'Tosha wagged her finger in Eve's direction. "Don't even front. You know you checking for 'em."

"Girl, bye. I'm not checking for anybody. Shit, I'm barely checking for myself. I can't even think about a man in my mix until I get my life back in order."

"Well, if I was you, I'd be checking for the print," said Na'Tosha.

Monique threw shade Na'Tosha's way. "Yeah... Checking for the strap-on print."

Eve laughed and almost spat out her drink.

Na'Tosha gave both ladies the middle finger. "Eff both y'all punk-rock beezys."

"Since we're already on the subject of strap-ons... How's Bo doing nowadays?" asked Monique.

"Why are you asking me? I don't know... What I do know is—I'm a month clean from all that drama and I ain't going back."

Eve was shocked. "A month now, huh? Girl, you're serious this time, aren't you?"

"Yeah, bitch I'm tired of playing. We ain't getting nowhere. Same ole shit over and over."

Monique chuckled. "You know what? You and Bo get on my damn nerves."

Na'Tosha dusted her hands off. "Locks changed and no more games. My New Year's resolution."

Monique laughed. "But, honey... It's the middle of May."

"And?" Na'Tosha raised her voice, "Don't come fa me. Better late than never."

Eve switched the topic, "Seriously... Thanks again for everything you both have done for me. I couldn't have gotten through this past year without y'all."

Na'Tosha hugged Eve. "Aww. You know we got you."

"Always, boo," added Monique.

Na'Tosha couldn't let the moment live. She just had to turn it into something else. "See... See... But I told ya ass to let me cut the nigga when you caught 'em sending dick pics to that frail ass, fake-titty-having

Becky wit' the blonde hair. But nooo—you wanted yo' marriage. You wanted to make shit work."

"Na'Tosha, stop it," yelled Monique.

"No, it's okay. She's right. I should've left then."

"As a matter of fact, what's the bitch's name again?" Na'Tosha snapped her fingers, "Jenny, Kelley, Stacy?"

"The home wrecking skank's name is Donna," said Eve.

Na'Tosha reached into her clutch, pulled out a small Beretta, and recklessly brandished it into the air. "Well, Donna finna get this work if I ever run into her ass again. And y'all know I keep that on me."

Monique grabbed the gun and shoved it back into Na'Tosha's clutch. "Girl, put that up."

The bartender approached the ladies shortly after. "Ready for another round?"

Eve ordered first, "Yes, I'll have another Long Island."

Monique went next. "Me as well... Thanks, hun."

And last, but not least, Na'Tosha, a.k.a. Ms. Always Extra said, "Give me a double shot of Henny, and make it stiff, boo."

"Damn girl, you're doubling up? I'm telling you now Na'Tosha, I'm not carrying you up all them steps tonight," said Eve.

"Girl, stop it. I'm finna turn this bitch up for you tonight." Na'Tosha twerked as Juvenile's "Back That Azz Up" came bursting through the speakers. "Heeeeyyy, this our shit. Come on y'all." Na'Tosha grabbed both ladies' hand and headed to the dance floor.

With her besties in front, and the divorce in the rear, the road to redemption looked promising for Eve.

"Hold that round for us, boo," yelled Eve, grinning at the bartender, as Na'Tosha dragged her away.

The bartender smiled. "I'm already on top of it."

CHAPTER TWO

Monique nearly tripped over her own two feet while stumbling into her downtown L.A., skyscraper office building. Her eyes were blood shot red and Triple Sec from her many Long Island Iced Teas reeked from her pores. A full night of partying with the girls left her hungover, hoarse, and sore from 'backing that ass up' into the wee hours of the night. An excruciating migraine made the morning even more miserable. She staggered through the hallways like a zombie, with a cup of coffee in one hand, and her briefcase in the other. While counting down the seconds until her fourth aspirin kicked in, Monique gave the "I'm not in the fuckin mood" stare down to anyone who dared to greet her. Most of her colleagues got the message except for an insubordinate nuisance that was Monique's receptionist.

Rebecca was a young Caucasian lady in her early twenties. She stood 5'8" with long, supermodel legs. Rebecca also had a tight bubble butt, great smile, and long red hair down to the middle of her back. Add in her perky size 36-C cup breasts, and you had every old white man's dream doll.

The problem was Monique couldn't stand Rebecca. And it was obvious that the feeling was mutual. There was no question that Rebecca was easy on the eyes. However, she was rude, immature, ditsy, and worst of all, privileged. Not to mention, the fact she was a home wrecker.

Monique hiring Rebecca wasn't a choice. It was actually a demand disguised as a favor for senior partner, Channing Froth. Rebecca was Mr. Froth's side piece and he expressed the need to keep a close eye on her without making his wife suspicious. The whole idea of it made Monique sick to her stomach, but she reminded herself that sometimes, in order to get where you want to go in life, you gotta do what you gotta do. That was Monique's way of not allowing her conscience to get the best of her. More importantly, it kept her from punching Rebecca in the face, like she'd envisioned on so many occasions.

Monique spotted Rebecca from the corner of her eye, seated at her desk on a phone call. She attempted to slip by, but Rebecca's radar was already zoned in.

She placed her call on hold and flagged Monique down. "Good morning, Monique. In your office—"

Monique corrected Rebecca mid-sentence. "—Excuse me... Did you just call me, Monique?"

Rebecca clinched her jaws, mirroring the snarl of an angry pit-bull, "Apologies... Ms. Harris. In your..."

Before Rebecca could utter another word, Monique was halfway to her office. Upon entering, she pivoted in Rebecca's direction. "Whatever it is, it will have to wait until I'm done with my coffee, hun." Monique childishly raised her coffee cup countering Rebecca's attitude with a little of her own.

"Whatever you say... Boss lady." Rebecca's mind filled with evil thoughts as Monique staggered into her office. She mumbled a few words that if heard, were sure to have gotten her fired.

Monique stepped through the door of her plush, corner view office to find the room filled with a multitude of beautiful, vibrant, sweet smelling roses. The bouquets of three hundred plus roses were carefully aligned, and color-coordinated throughout the entire office.

Monique stood frozen. "What... The... F—" She caught herself before cursing.

On top of her desk was a heartfelt note:

> Here are a dozen roses for every day that it's been since I've heard the sound of your beautiful voice. Hope to hear from you soon.
>
> - Mario

"Wow. He really went all in." She nodded her head. "Impressive." Monique took a few minutes to observe the remarkable display. "Maybe I should unblock him—nah."

Monique and Mario met a couple months prior at a Black-Tie Gala in Calabasas. Mr. Froth brought her as his guest, displaying her amongst the "Who's Who" of L.A. County like a token black prize. It didn't bother Monique because she used it as an opportunity to network with some of the west coast's biggest corporate moguls. Mr. Froth jokingly introduced Mario as the next big solar tycoon. The attraction was instant between the two so they exchanged information and communicated regularly.

Monique learned that not only was he tall, handsome, educated, and cemented into a thriving career, but he also had a beautiful penthouse overlooking Pershing Square, drove a brand new Rolls-Royce, and didn't have any children. To the average woman, he was a gift, wrapped, sealed, and delivered from God. After going on a couple dates, Monique vanished. Something about Mario's unrealistic image left her skeptical.

She logged into her laptop. A notification reminded her that it was date night with her grandmother. "Shit. Tonight is bingo night with Grandmommy. How did I forget that?" Monique texted Eve to cancel their evening plans.

> MONIQUE: Hey, what ya doin?
> EVE: Working... Guess what tho? I got my keys!
> MONIQUE: Yaaass, girl. Won't He do it?

EVE: Thanks for hiring the movers. I'll give you the money when I see you.
MONIQUE: You're welcome. Consider it a house warming gift.
EVE: Aww. Thanks boo!!! What time are you falling through tonight?
Monique: I can't tonight. I've got a bingo date with Grandmommy. Totally forgot. My bad
EVE: No worries. I've got it covered from here. You've done way more than enough. Tell Ms. Ida I said heeeyy, guuurrll. lol
MONIQUE: Sure will hun lol.

Rebecca appeared in the door way. "Ms. Harris, your eight o'clock is here."

"Rebecca, can you please explain to me why you didn't tell me that I had a whole garden of roses in my office?"

Rebecca's eyes lit up at the opportunity to fire a slick jab at her superior. "Actually, that's what I tried to tell you as soon as you dragged in this morning." Rebecca smiled.

This was one of those times when Monique wanted to knock Rebecca's teeth out. Instead of throwing a punch, as well as her career away, Monique opted to just throw Rebecca out of her office. "Please, let Mr. Okohana know that I'll be out in just a second, and make sure to close the door behind you."

"Yes, Your Highness. I'll also be sure to contact maintenance about taking care of this beautiful little mess you have going on in here." Rebecca rolled her eyes on the way out.

"Monique, why haven't you fired her yet? Oh, yeah... Because she's bangin' your boss. That's why... Duh," Monique whispered to herself after Rebecca slammed the door.

She surveyed the room. Roses covered nearly every inch. Monique would never admit it out loud, but Rebecca was right. Her office was indeed one, big, beautiful mess

CHAPTER THREE

Na'Tosha casually filed her nails and smacked on gum. She was leaning against the cherry red accent wall positioned next to the front door of her Inglewood apartment as if she didn't have a single worry in the world. Or did she? Bo, her on again, off again girlfriend of four plus years was on the other side pleading for another chance.

In Na'Tosha's mind, there wasn't anything left to discuss. Bo was no different than the men that preceded her. She'd proven to be a habitual liar, cheater, and certified scrub for the majority of their relationship. Na'Tosha hoped that things would change when she decided to date someone of the same sex. She couldn't have been more wrong.

Na'Tosha had occasionally experimented with women in her younger days. Partying all night on Hennessy and Molly landed her in some peculiar positions. Yet, this was her first, actual, committed relationship with a female.

Beyond the tough persona, Bo wasn't bad looking. She had a caramel complexion, with long, sandy-brown hair she kept in two neat French braids. Bo dressed in all the latest designer trends and was known to keep a fresh pair of kicks on her feet.

The area of 108th street and Figueroa was Bo's stomping grounds. She proudly wore the affiliation in ink all over her body. She was down for whatever when it came to the gang, but often came up short in regard to her relationship with Na'Tosha. In the beginning, she dazzled Na'Tosha with loads of money and exotic gifts. But Bo failed to consistently pull her weight as time progressed.

Unfortunately, Na'Tosha trusted Bo with a little more than just her heart. At one point, she'd also made the dreaded mistake of giving her access to all of her credit cards. Na'Tosha fell into the class of women who felt obligated to be a "ride or die" through their significant other's inability to provide.

Shortly after opening her salon, "Small But Chic Beauty Parlor," Bo had gotten ahold of her social security number. Her heavy clientele, combined with the booth rent she charged the other five stylists, pulled in a nice amount of cash. But most of it went towards bills and debt accumulated by Bo's irresponsible spending habits. Na'Tosha couldn't wait to get rid of Bo and straighten her credit out so she could finally start saving money again. Sadly, Bo just wouldn't leave her alone. Every time it seemed like she'd gotten her out of her system, Bo would show right back up at the door like a sad puppy dog.

After years of the same pattern of behavior, Na'Tosha had finally had enough.

The problem was Bo hadn't quite gotten the memo. "Please, baby open the door... I'm sorry. Just hear me out."

"I'm hearing yo' ass out, all right—right the fuck out of my life."

"Baby, why are you doing me like this? After all the shit we've been through. This is how you gon' do me?" Bo banged on the door. "It's cold out here. Baby, come on just open the door."

"I don't have time for this. I'm trying to get ready for work, and yo' ass know good and damn well it ain't cold outside. Nigga, it's clearly eighty degrees... The fuck."

Bo went with the first excuse that came to mind. "Quit playing you know that I'm anemic. I didn't take my iron pills today. Baby, open the door... Damn."

"Oh, well. Take ya ass back to Tonya house. That's probably where ya damn iron pills at."

"Tonya?" Bo paused, "You mean Tiana?"

Na'Tosha kicked the door as hard as she could. "Tramp, you know who the fuck I'm talking about. While you're sitting over here correcting me about this bitch name. See, you know what..."

"Okay, okay. Baby, I'm sorry. It's not even like that. Just let me in. I promise I'll do right this time."

"Nope. All ya shit is in trash bags at ya mammy house. You ain't got nothin' left over here, boo boo... Now, crawl ya tired, good-for-nothing ass back to Tanaka."

"Please, baby," cried Bo.

"Damn, nigga stop begging. Man up. Woman up. Or whatever the hell you refer to yourself as. Just make sure you do it on ya way to wherever you're going."

Bo pounded on Na'Tosha's door. "Bitch, you got me fucked up. Open up the door. This is my house too."

"Bitch? Seriously, Bo? You know what? I'm not finna play with you. Nigga, I'm calling your P.O." Na'Tosha retrieved her phone from the coffee table. "Yep. You know what? That's exactly what I'm gon' do. Yo' ass is going to jail today."

Bo paced back and forth in front of the door as Na'Tosha dialed away. She lowered her voice, "All right, all right. You win, I'm leaving... Just let me get my PlayStation, and I'm gone."

"PlayStation? Ha. Yeah, okay... You gon' play the crying game... On yo' way to the police station. That's the only PlayStation you're getting up out of here."

Bo made one last attempt to play on Na'Tosha's feelings for her. "Baby, why are you tripping like this? I can't believe you're just going to throw four years away like that."

"No, you threw four years away... I'm just throwing ya PlayStation away."

Na'Tosha carefully disconnected the console from behind the television and tossed it out the window. "Now, go tell Tania to buy ya trifling ass a new one."

Bo exited the premises with her head down, punching the air. With her relationship in shambles, and now her freedom in question, Bo's L.A. sunshine, turned into a Seattle rainy day in as quick as a New York minute.

CHAPTER FOUR

Eve was relieved to finally be able to unwind after working a full shift, fighting mid-day traffic, getting the kids settled, as well as unpacking boxes. The opportunity to relax had been long overdue. For the past year or so, she had been dealing with a bitter divorce that uncovered more than her poor heart could handle. The chance for a brand-new start presented so much promise. But, the skeletons of the past still lurked near and dear to the core.

Things weren't always bad during her and now ex-husband Deshaun's ten-year tenure. At one point, the college sweethearts were inseparable. Once Eve got pregnant with D.J., during the end of their junior year, Deshaun put his education on hold and got a job working at his grandfather's auto body shop. Eve swore to never leave his side after watching him sacrifice his own degree in order for her to complete hers.

Shortly after she graduated, the two had a small wedding and moved into a tiny apartment located in a rough area known as Baldwin Village. Eve got a job working at a bank and together the newlyweds worked countless hours to provide for their new family. The plan was to save enough for a down payment on a house. And afterwards, Deshaun would go back and finish his final year of school. She loved that he was so excited about getting his degree and pursuing his dream of becoming a film director. The idea of accomplishing these goals even helped him persevere through two years of working a minimum of sixty hours a week. Eve admired her husband's work ethic and ambition. She always smiled as his eyes brightened with great passion when speaking about his future in the film industry.

Three years later, they moved into their new house. The excitement from being first time homeowners, and Deshaun's acceptance into the University of California Los Angeles' prestigious film program, filled every square inch of their beautiful new home. Right before Deshaun's spring semester debut at UCLA, Eve had more great news. She was pregnant with the couple's second child. Initially, Deshaun was filled with joy. They'd always talked about having another baby, just not so soon.

After realizing that he'd have to put his dreams on hold again—or even give them up for good, Eve noticed Deshaun's behavior starting to change. Instead of going back to school, Deshaun continued to work. He stayed out late, partying all the time and drinking a lot more than usual. In the beginning, Eve didn't think much of it. But after she found a white, powdered substance and a condom in the dirty clothes hamper, she knew that there was a serious problem. When she confronted Deshaun, he reluctantly admitted to the cocaine but denied sleeping with other women. He also used reverse psychology by accusing Eve of getting pregnant on purpose and deliberately ruining his dreams. Although Eve knew that those allegations weren't true, she did feel a level of guilt for the unexpected conceiving of their newborn child. So, she decided to forgive him, thinking that prayer and a little counseling would eventually make things go back to normal.

Things got worse as time progressed. Deshaun's foul behavior became bolder with every year that passed. Eve didn't know what to do. The cheating, drugs, and liquor was bad, but the domestic violence made things even worse. Some nights, Deshaun would come home drunk, high, and smelling like other women's perfume. This would lead to arguments that would usually end with him pounding away at her face.

Eve's perfect husband had turned into an abusive, two-timing, coke-sniffing demon. Still, she had faith that one day this animal would change back into the loving man that she married. Eve was faced with the tough decision of either staying and praying her way through it or leaving and starting over as a single mother of two. Sadly, Deshaun would eventually cross an unforgiveable barrier that made the decision a lot easier than before.

The initial steps of moving forward had officially begun. Eve, the children, and the dog moved a few miles east of the El Segundo home that she and Deshaun built together. Unlike the two-story, four-bedroom, twenty-eight hundred square foot Victorian-style house, Eve's new cozy, two-bedroom, dingbat-styled apartment provided the sense of freedom and independence that she so desperately needed.

It wasn't hard to see that it was a major downgrade from what they were accustomed to. Friends and family often questioned why she forfeited the house so easily. Regardless of the size, Eve no longer saw value in the home or anything inside of it, for that matter. She could care less about the material things. If anything, it was all a constant reminder of Deshaun's despicable ways. Her only concern was making sure that the children hadn't shown any psychological issues stemming from the abrupt chain of events. As long as Eve knew her babies were good, she'd manage. Nonetheless, a long journey of self-healing was still ahead.

The heavy burden of dealing with divorce had been removed. But trauma from all the years of abuse, at the hands of a man once considered her king, still remained. After all, this was the person she exchanged vows with and bared children for. The physical scars from Deshaun's intoxicated tirades were healed. It was the ongoing verbal mistreatment that left dark clouds of doubt and uncertainty.

Any man in his right mind could look at Eve and see her beauty. Her radiant, milk chocolate skin was filled with melanin. A luscious set of full lips, and high cheek bones, superbly accented her deep, adorable dimples. Eve was also blessed with a head full of thick, healthy, natural hair...

Nevertheless, she was the mother of two, and with that came certain changes to her physique. The 5'7" lean frame she once possessed wasn't there anymore. Eve did her best to exercise and eat healthy. Unfortunately, some of the stubborn baby weight just refused to go away, and Deshaun reminded her of it every chance he got. What Eve hadn't lost in pounds, was certainly lost in confidence.

It was approximately 11 p.m. and the kids were sound asleep. Eve wrapped her hair in a towel and applied a facial mask. The smooth, sensual sound of Debarge's "All This Love" played through the portable

Bluetooth speaker. She turned off the lights and lit six scented candles sitting around the edge of the bathtub. Then, Eve grabbed a bottle of wine she placed at the side of the bath tub, pouring a glass of Pinot to secure the vibe. Next, Eve positioned herself into the steamy bubble bath. The scorching hot water soothed her entire body. Operation "max and relax" was in full effect.

"All the boxes are unpacked... I've got the kid's lunches hooked up for school tomorrow... Their clothes are ironed... Yaaasss. Now it's Mommy's time." Eve sunk deeply into the tub, carefully grabbing the glass of wine, and taking a sip. "Thank you, Jesus for turning water into wine." Suddenly her phone rang. "This better not be anybody but Jesus himself calling to say, 'you're welcome.'"

"Hello?"

"Good evening, Eve. It's Quentin."

Eve couldn't control the urge to blush. She took a moment to gather herself before replying.

"Hello, Coach Nelson—don't you think it's a little late?"

"I'm sorry. I didn't mean to disturb you. I was just concerned about D.J. missing the last couple of practices. Is everything okay?"

"Yes, everything is fine. We were in the process of moving, but now that we're situated, it shouldn't be an issue."

"Great. Awesome. Congrats on the move."

"Thanks. We're all excited about the new start. It was definitely much needed."

"I bet. What side of town are you on now?"

"We're in Hawthorne."

"Hawthorne? That's great. I'm right next door in Gardena. As a matter of fact, I can pick DJ up and drop him off if that'll help."

Although his gesture was kind, it was a little too forward for Eve. *"Thanks, but that won't be necessary."*

"Oh, okay... Well, I won't hold you. I just wanted you to know that D.J. is a great kid, and one of our best players. He has so much potential. If there's anything I can do to lighten your load—I mean in regard to D.J. and basketball, of course, feel free to give me a call."

"Thanks, Quentin. I'll definitely keep that in mind. Good night."

"Good night, Eve."

Eve knew that Coach Nelson's concerns for D.J. were sincere. He'd been his AAU basketball coach for the past two seasons and always went out of his way to show his support. She could also tell that he had a slight crush on her. Even though she was flattered to have a guy, almost ten years her junior, admire her, she'd never cross that boundary. For one, he was just a baby, still wet behind the ears. And most importantly, she'd never want to shame D.J. by putting him in an awkward position like that.

There wasn't any chance of Eve becoming his cougar, but it didn't stop her from partaking in a little flirtation. Her and Coach Nelson would often joke around as the kid's practiced. She couldn't ignore the fact that he was a handsome dark brown 6'2", bearded, three-sixty wave wearing coach. Yet, Eve still wasn't tempted to cross that threshold. That didn't stop her from having fantasies though.

"Coach Nelson better watch out calling me all late like that." Eve took another sip of wine. "Wit' his fine ass—ah, he's just so young." She fanned herself. "Girl, get yourself together. A man should be the last thing on your mind right now."

Coach Nelson's voice sent Eve's mind spiraling into the gutter. Her vagina throbbed at the thought of him digging inside of her. She visualized his tongue twirling against her clitoris. The wine was definitely getting the best of her.

"Where's my damn vibrator?" Eve reached over the side of the tub and grabbed her trusty little friend. The small, silicon vibrating bullet was always within arm's reach during bath time. Being the mother of two young, nosey kids meant "rubbing one off" whenever the opportunity presented itself. Eve placed it underneath the water and pleasured herself. The fantasy of Coach Nelson dishing out oral pleasure, sent chills down her spine. Eve's moans became louder as her body trembled. Her eyes rolled back into her head, as a climax was on the horizon. "Coach Nelson, don't stop, daddy. I'm cummin. I'm cummin, daddy. Don't stop." Eve's shoulders tensed and her legs trembled. She was seconds away from the ultimate explosion. Her toes curled as she braced herself for the finale. "Here I come."

Seconds later the doorknob wiggled. Eve's daughter Denisha stormed into the bathroom unannounced. She flicked the light switch and shielded her eyes from the brightness.

Eve's heart dropped. The last thing she needed was for her seven-year-old daughter to see mommy getting off. Eve frantically tossed the vibrator into a mini trashcan located next to the toilet.

"Yes, what's the problem, sweetheart?"

Denisha wiped her eyes. "I had a bad dream."

The vibrator gyrated inside of the trashcan, slowly moving it towards the door.

"Mommy, why is the trashcan shaking?"

Eve hopped up quickly and wrapped herself in a towel. "Baby, you must be tired. That's only your imagination. Mommy will be out in just a second. Okay?"

Eve hurried Denisha out of the bathroom. Her heart raced faster than a greyhound on steroids. "I can't even take a damn bath in peace." She pressed her back against the door and slid down to the floor before pouting. "Lord Jesus, I need a vacation." Operation "max and relax" was officially over.

CHAPTER FIVE

"Knock, knock. Good morning, Grandmommy," said Monique as she entered the door to her grandmother's convalescent quarters. She handed her a Styrofoam container filled with her favorite morning dish. Chicken and waffles often provided a level of comfort for both of them throughout the years. The unconventional southern dish consistently brought warmth in moments of despair.

The origin of this despair began for Monique at a very early age. Her parents tragically died in a car accident when she was only three years old. A police cruiser speeding through oncoming traffic struck the couple's vehicle, killing them instantly. The untimely death of Monique's parents brought deep devastation to the entire family. Through it all, Monique was blessed to have an outstanding woman step forward and fill the void to the best of her ability.

Ida Mae Jenkins, affectionately known as Grandmommy, was the only mother Monique knew. Tough, unfiltered, and straight forward was the best way to describe her. She gave respect to all and commanded it in return. If Ida Mae loved you, she'd give you the shirt off her back. But if Ida Mae didn't love you, she'd snatch the shirt off your back, and it give to someone she did love. That's just the way Ida Mae operated.

Monique naturally adopted that same zero tolerance, no nonsense mentality. That way of thinking was effective in regard to her career as a stockbroker. Monique just wished it produced the same results in regard to her love life.

"Aww, bless yo' heart, baby. You didn't have to bring me this."

"Stop it, Grandmommy. You know you're my favorite girl."

Ida Mae opened the container revealing her favorite breakfast treat. "You sure know how to make a girl feel good, don't ya?"

Monique smiled while taking off her jacket. She loved being able to bring joy to her grandmother. She sat beside Ida Mae and carefully poured syrup onto the perfectly griddled, golden brown waffles. "I had so much fun at bingo last night. But, umm... Imma need you to stop cheat-ing okay, Ms. Thang? You're going to mess around and get us kicked out."

Ida Mae smiled. "Baby, you know the rules... It's only cheating if you get caught."

"You are too much."

"Too much? Your paw-paw used to say that I was just right." Ida Mae patted her hair in an attempt to look sexy.

"Girl, I'm scared of you," said Monique.

"Girl, you better be." Ida Mae always knew how to make Monique laugh.

Monique shifted the attention towards an old, wrinkled photo of a young gentleman wearing a uniform. "Look at Paw-Paw when he was in the Army."

"Yes, baby. He was so fine... Lord knows how much I miss that man."

"I know you do... I miss him, too."

"Fifty... Seven... Years of marriage, and I wouldn't trade one single minute of it."

"Wow, that's a long time... I couldn't even imagine being with a man that long."

"Why not?" asked Ida Mae.

"Because things are just different nowadays. Picture-perfect, fairy-tale marriages like back in your day don't exist anymore."

Ida Mae laughed. "Picture perfect? Sweetie, our marriage was far from perfect. As a matter of fact, it was a thirteen-year span where I hated his guts."

"Thirteen years? Are you serious?"

"Might've been even longer if my memory serves me right."

Monique was confused. She'd always viewed her grandparent's marriage as the ultimate union. "What happened? What did he do?"

"Be a man... You name it—he did it."

Hearing of a period when her grandfather was misbehaving completely threw her for a loop. "Grandmommy... Why didn't you just leave?"

"Leave? And go find a different man? Just to deal with a whole new set of problems?"

"No. Go find a man who would've treated you better."

Ida Mae placed her hand onto Monique's shoulder. "Baby, any man you decide to be with is going to need some work. Men are prideful, lustful, and some just plain ole dumbful. If you're sitting around hoping for Mr. Picture Perfect to roll around, you're going to be old and dried up waiting for 'em ... And guess what?"

"What?" asked Monique.

"He still ain't gon' come."

"Un uhh... I'm sorry—I ain't gon' be able to do it."

Ida Mae tapped Monique's thigh. "Child, hush."

"I'm serious... I don't want to give my heart to the wrong one."

"Baby listen... Your paw-paw gave me the best years of my life. Together we made a lifetime full of memories. Sure, there were some dark days, but guess what? We made it through. And together we created many years of sunshine. Trust me... Your Mr. Right is out there somewhere... But Mr. Picture Perfect doesn't exist."

Monique's stubbornness wouldn't allow her to fully agree. "I guess you could be right."

"Oh hush, child... You'll be fine. Now go out there and make me some great grand babies."

"Now hold up... I didn't say all that."

"Well, why not? What the hell are you waiting on?"

"I mean... Of course, I want a family, but definitely not right now. I have goals that I need to accomplish in my career first."

"Child, you better go and make them babies. If I was your age, I'd be given it up all the time."

Monique was disgusted. "Ewww, no. Please, stop."

Ida Mae was just getting started. "I'm talking 'bout bumpin', humpin', pumpin', thumpin' all over the place, baby."

Monique interpreted this as her que to leave. Sitting around listening to her eighty-year-old grandmother talk about sex wasn't a part of her day's plan. "Yikes. Look at the time... Okay, Grandmommy. Gotta go. Gonna be late for work... Love you... Muah."

Monique kissed Ida Mae on the forehead. She grabbed her purse and jacket before heading out. To her surprise, Ida Mae still wasn't done.

"I'm talking good lovin', body-rockin' knockin' boots all night long."

Monique smiled as she exited the room.

Ida Mae was indeed a cold piece of work, but her knowledge and wisdom was second to none. Her health was gradually declining, and it was only a matter of time before the inevitable occurred. Monique dreaded the thought of living without her. She did her best to block those thoughts. Moments like these were too special to take for granted.

Ida Mae's advice persuaded Monique to do something that she'd wrestled with for days. She scrolled through her text threads until she landed on a certain individual and typed a message.

Monique: Hey Mario, it's been a while... Thanks for the beautiful roses.

CHAPTER SIX

Na'Tosha absolutely hated going to the mall. Department store clothing never seemed to fit her properly. All the cute jeans were either too tight in the thighs, or extremely loose in the waist. The tops were just as bad. They either didn't adjust well enough to her breasts or flanked out at the bottom. If it was up to her, she'd just strut around naked all day.

The clothes at the mall were only half the problem. Na'Tosha also had to deal with the eye-hawking spectators of the world. Men of all races stared regardless of what she was wearing. Young, old, single, married it didn't matter. Even women admired her assets from afar. Some hated, others congratulated. All in all, they stared.

Na'Tosha wouldn't be caught dead inside of Fox Hills Mall if it wasn't for Eve's son, D.J. His birthday was approaching, and the pair of shoes he requested was sold out online. Her last attempt to find these exclusive sneakers meant going into one of the busiest malls in America. Let's just say, she wasn't too happy about it.

A gauntlet of thirsty creeps lined both sides of the walkway leading to the shoe store. Na'Tosha wasn't in the mood for the catcalls and whack game spitting. She hoped that if her eyes remained focused directly ahead, then maybe they'd get the message. The group of men wasted no time.

"Damn baby, can I holla at you for a second?"

"Nah, I'm good," she responded.

"What's up, sexy? What's your name?"

"Sorry, ain't got one."

"Aye ma, come here. Check it out real quick."

"Sorry, I'm married." Na'Tosha kept moving.

"I don't see no ring," another dude said.

"It's in the pawn shop."

"Let me help you get it out then."

"No thanks."

Na'Tosha blocked every attempt with the poise of a seasoned veteran. She scurried into the shoe store flabbergasted by the last guy's offer. "Did this man just say he'll help me get my wedding ring out of the pawn shop? Thirsty niggas these days, I tell ya."

Na'Tosha spotted the shoes. Shortly after, she was approached by what appeared to be more unwanted attention.

"Excuse me, can I help you with—" started the gentleman, before being rudely interrupted.

"—Nigga, I'm not interested. Can a bitch shop in peace? The Fuck," yelled Na'Tosha.

"Just checking to see if I could help you with anything?"

Na'Tosha turned and locked eyes with the uniformed employee. She immediately noticed how handsome he was, and then his name tag: Chaz. Na'Tosha wasn't the type to get sprung off a dude, but there was something about him that had her mesmerized.

She smiled, gazing deeply into his green eyes. "Depends on what you wanna help me with."

Chaz was slightly confused. "What size are you looking for?"

"Big—biiigg sizes only, boo."

"Umm, okay... You mean like a twelve?"

"Bigger."

"Thirteen?"

Na'Tosha licked her lips and stretched her hands far apart from one another.

"Bigger."

"We are talking about shoes, right?"

"Maybe... Maybe not," Na'Tosha was totally out of character. While gawking at Chaz, an inner voice spoke to her, *Look at yo' ass in here thirsty. You better shake back. This man is a whole shoe salesman. Hoe, if you don't get yo' life. Now snap yo' ass back.*

Na'Tosha slowly shook her head and snapped back into reality. She'd often had spells where voices took control of her mind, but never in relation to a man. Na'Tosha took a few seconds to regain her composure.

"Hey, are you okay?" asked Chaz.

"Homie, back up out my fuckin' face."

"Hey—it's all good..." He backed up with his palms raised. "Calm down—do you still want the shoes?"

"Size six, nigga. And hurry yo' ass up. I got somewhere to be."

Chaz scratched his head after going to grab the shoes. "Her ass got some serious issues."

Na'Tosha watched as Chaz disappeared into the back. "Ole cute, sexy broke ass. Had me all out of pocket just now. Panties all wet and shit. I don't even like light skinned niggas. Knowing good and damn well I don't got time for no minimum wage beige."

CHAPTER SEVEN

It was 6:45 a.m. and Eve was running late. Long nights and early mornings were just a part of her daily routine. This was something Eve had grown accustomed to since separating from her ex-husband. He had the luxury of dropping off fancy gifts, coming and going as he pleased, as well as portraying the image of being the fun parent. Eve, on the other hand, was stuck with the everyday, primary parenting duties. She handled the important stuff that kids didn't seem to appreciate until they went off on their own.

Eve hated the fact that Deshaun had it so easy. It irked her soul to watch him move around freely. He partied all night long, traveled whenever he wanted, and posted every little thing he did for the kids all over social media. Meanwhile, Eve was left to do all the grunt work. It wasn't fair, but at the end of the day, it was her reality. There wasn't anything on earth that Eve wouldn't do for her children. So, she did what any good mother would, tucked her feelings into her back pocket and made do.

She pulled into the parking lot of the kid's school at exactly 8:35 a.m. The tardy bell rang as she put the car in park. "Come on y'all, hurry up."

D.J. and Denisha unbuckled their seatbelts and rushed out of the car.

Eve ushered the kids to the front door where she was greeted by the principal.

"Good morning, Mrs. Nelson."

"Good morning, Mrs. Clarkson. I'm sorry they're late. We had a rough start this morning and traffic was terrible."

"May I have a word with you, please?"

"Sure... Of course." Eve kissed both children on the forehead. "Have a great day, all right?"

The children nodded their heads in compliance and headed towards their respective classes.

Eve took in a deep breath as Mrs. Clarkson paced along the row of lockers. "Is everything okay?"

Mrs. Clarkson locked her arms behind her back while doing her best not to make eye contact. "Unfortunately, things aren't as well as I'd like them to be... Your children's tuition is past due sixty days now."

"How is that possible? Their father submits the payment monthly online, the same as he did last year."

"Umm... Yes... About that... We've contacted Mr. Nelson numerous times, and he seems to never be available. We've left several messages, to no avail. Well, until yesterday that is... Mr. Nelson stated that he would no longer be responsible for the payments, and in fact, you would be taking over from here on out." Mrs. Clarkson handed Eve a white envelope with an invoice for the amount of $3,308.63.

"Now Mrs. Nelson, I hate to inform you of this under these circumstances, but St. Joseph's Preparatory policy is to terminate any student's enrollment if tuition exceeds a sixty-day delinquency. With that being said, I'm willing to extend it out for an additional week, but that's the best that I can do. Anything beyond that will leave me with no other choice but to terminate their enrollment immediately."

Eve knew that Deshaun was the king of being spiteful and petty. Nevertheless, she didn't see this one coming. This was his children's education at stake. How could he do something so evil?

Eve managed to forge a smile before responding to Mrs. Clarkson, "I completely understand. It'll get it taken care of... Thank you, Mrs. Clarkson."

"You're welcome... Take care of yourself."

Mrs. Clarkson made her way towards her office, leaving Eve in deep thought.

Deshaun had done a lot of hurtful things over the years, but this one took the cake. Eve's embarrassment turned into anger. The only thing on her mind was payback.

In the past, she'd contemplated murdering him in several ways. Shooting, stabbing, suffocating, and running him over with a big rig, w-ere all common occurrences inside of Eve's head. But the consequences were too steep. She couldn't fathom being locked up and away from her children. However, Deshaun not doing his part was beginning to weigh on her conscience. Somehow, he always found a way to leave her picking up the pieces and she was sick of it.

Eve left the school with her four-inch Steve Madden heels tapping loudly against the tile floors. She marched towards the exit ready to whoop Deshaun's ass.

"This muthafucka really tried it this time."

All the prayer in the world wouldn't have swayed her. She dialed his number the moment her hand pushed against the double doors.

CHAPTER 8
THE PHONE CALL

Deshaun noticed his phone ringing. "Who the hell is this calling me so damn early?" He was still in bed recovering from a long night of partying. His former mistress, Donna, nestled beside him. Apparently, she'd been upgraded to girlfriend status. Sadly, it was only by default. Deshaun manipulated her poor little white mind every chance he could. In his eyes, she was nothing more than a walking, talking ATM. Donna never talked back, questioned his whereabouts, or nagged him about anything. She was a woman without a voice, and that was exactly the way his narcissistic mind preferred it.

After letting the phone ring a few times, Deshaun finally answered. *"Yo?"*

"Deshaun, I'm at the school, and they're saying that the tuition is past due," said Eve.

"Okay, then pay it."

"You know good and damn well I don't have no thirty-three hundred dollars for these people."

"Well, according to the state of California, I only have to pay six-hundred a month... So, that's all I'm paying."

"How are you just going to decide that you're not paying their tuition anymore? Forget whatever we have going on. This is your kids's education that we're talking about."

"Put 'em in public school then. They'll be all right. Shit, it was good enough for me and you."

"No, we agreed to never put them in public school. Or did you forget about that the same way you forgot about your wedding vows?"

"Welp... Shit changed when you filed for divorce and put them white folks in our business."

Eve's voice cracked, *"You were cheating on me, Deshaun. Dogging me out left and right. Putting your hands on me whenever you got bored. What was I supposed to do? I caught you over and over and you still kept doing it. And after the last bullshit with the nurse—"*

"—Last. Past. Kiss my ass. Why are we still talking about old shit? What's done is done now get out of your feelings."

Eve could hear a woman's voice in the background, saying, *"Babe, is everything okay?"*

"Bitch, mind yo' fucking business and go back to sleep," said Deshaun with conviction.

"Let me guess... You're laid up with that little white trick right now? So, that's why you're acting brand new?"

"That's no longer your concern. Plus, don't get it twisted... This bitch ain't nobody. She know what's up. Instead of worrying about who I'm laid up with, you need to concentrate on getting that tuition taken care of."

"I should've seen this coming a long time ago."

Deshaun laughed. *"It is what it is. You'll figure it out. I have faith in you."*

"I can't believe you're doing this right now."

"So, what... Tough titty... Life ain't fair. Deal with it."

"You're such an asshole."

"Come on now, Eve... I've been called worse by better. You have to come harder than that, sweetheart."

"It's all right tho'. I'll figure it out. Just like I always do." She wiped a lone tear rolling down her cheek.

Deshaun smiled. *"They're you go, champ... That's the spirit."*

"I hate yo' ass, Deshaun."

"Love you too, baby... Goodbye."

Deshaun tossed the phone on the floor.

Donna used this as an opportunity to ease his mind. She ducked underneath the covers and tried to suck him off.

"Move, bitch. I told yo' dumb ass about being all in my damn mouth while I'm on the phone," yelled Deshaun.

"Sorry babe, it won't happen again."

"It better not. Now, go fix me something to eat. I'm hungry."

Donna accepted her tongue lashing and proceeded to the kitchen. *"Whatever you say, babe."*

CHAPTER NINE

"Knock knock, hoe. Open the doe," yelled Na'Tosha at the top of her lungs.

Monique laughed while gripping a bottle of Eve's favorite wine.

The two were stopping by to christen Eve's new place in their typical alcohol-fueled fashion.

Eve opened the door and immediately snatched the bottle from Monique's hand. She was more excited to see the Pinot than the actual patrons who brought it.

"Well, hey to you too, lush," said Monique.

"Girl, bye. Y'all come on in."

The ladies entered Eve's apartment and took a look around.

"This is nice," said Na'Tosha.

Monique seconded that sentiment, "I like, sis... And this furniture."

"Yaaass. Cute, girl," added Na'Tosha.

"Y'all so sweet... I had to do something after Deadbeat D sold the other set."

Na'Tosha threw her hands on her hips. "Hold up, he did what?"

"Yes, girl. The flat-screens, dining room set, washer, dryer, refrigerator... He even sold the kid's trampoline."

"That sorry mutha..." Monique caught herself before cursing.

Na'Tosha gladly finished her sentence, "Fucka. Sorry mutha-fucka. She can't curse, but I sho can. The fuck."

"The sad part is, even after doing all that, I still thought that he might've had some level of decency left, but after what he did today..." Eve hesitated on whether to tell the ladies about what had happened at the school earlier.

To her benefit, the kids came storming in from their room.

"Auntie Mo... Auntie Na'Tosha."

Na'Tosha sucked her teeth and said, "Umm... Don't be saying her name first." She then laughed, reaching out to tickle them.

Monique playfully snapped back. "Excuse me?"

Both kids laughed. They always got a kick out of the way Monique and Na'Tosha interacted. Denisha clutched onto Monique's leg, while D.J. and Na'Tosha performed an elaborate handshake.

"Well, I'll be damned... Na'Tosha, how'd you remember all that?"

"Okay now, there you go cursing again," said Eve.

Monique rolled her eyes. "Damn isn't a curse word. It's in the Bible."

"So was hoes, killas, rapists, and snakes trickin' bitches into eating forbidden fruits and shit. But that don't make it right, now do it?" asked Na'Tosha.

"Na'Tosha," shouted Monique while motioning towards the children.

"I'm sorry, babies. Y'all know Tee-Tee Tosha mouth get a lil' ratchet sometimes."

"Yeah, we know," said Denisha.

Monique shook her head. "That's a shame."

"I said my bad, bitch, damn." Na'Tosha immediately covered her mouth.

Eve gave her the side-eye. "Hey, y'all go get ready for bed, and let us grown-ups finish our conversation."

"Awww," said Denisha.

"Good night, Auntie Mo... Good night, Tee-Tee Tosha," yelled D.J. on the way to the room.

Na'Tosha bent over and blew D.J. a kiss. He blushed as he caught the air kiss and placed it on his cheek.

"That's my boo right there," said Na'Tosha.

Eve smacked her lips. "He thinks he's your man."

"Closest thing she had to a man in years," added Monique.

Na'Tosha licked her tongue out at Monique while giving her the middle finger.

Eve laughed. "Hey, guess what? It's wine time."

Monique and Na'Tosha agreed, "Come through, wine time."

"Y'all are not going to believe what happened to me the other day," said Monique.

"Details," screamed Eve from the kitchen.

"I limped into work the day after Eve's shindig, got into my office, turned the lights on and bam. There's a million roses scattered all over the place... Well three-hundred and sixty to be exact."

"Were they from Mario?" asked Eve.

"Girl, yes."

Eve handed the ladies their drinks. "Aww. That was so sweet of him."

Monique grinned from ear to ear. "It was. He even left a little cute card on top of my desk."

Na'Tosha sipped her wine before letting her inner gold-digger pour out.

"Cute card? Was it from Saks? They gift cards are hella cute."

Eve laughed while Monique stared in disappointment.

"What? The card wasn't from Saks?"

Eve and Monique both shouted, "No."

"Was it from Neiman's? Their gift cards are cute too."

"No," Monique replied.

"Gucci?"

Eve and Monique shouted even louder, "No"

"Okay. Damn. My bad... Shit, them the kind of cards I call cute." Na'Tosha sipped her wine and shrugged her shoulders. "I don't know what y'all talkin' 'bout."

"Mo, please don't pay this heffa no mind... That was so thoughtful of him."

Monique's face glowed. "I know, right? That was the nicest thing a man has ever done for me."

"So... Did you call him?" asked Na'Tosha.

Monique took a huge gulp of wine. "I thanked him for flowers—the next day—through text."

"Monique," yelled Eve.

"I know, I know. I have to do better."

Na'Tosha offered a word of advice. "Well, whateva you do, don't give him none. If he doin' all that now… Just imagine how he gon' act after you put a lil' coochie on his face."

Monique and Eve stared.

"What did I say wrong now?" asked Na'Tosha.

"Anyways…" said Eve. "You need to call him. Girl, give him a chance."

"That's the same thing Grandmommy said."

Na'Tosha laughed. "Now, if we're talkin' 'bout the same Grandmommy that I know, I guarantee she said something about you putting coochie on him, in some form or fashion."

"Girl, you know she did."

"One time, me and Bo were in the area, so we stopped by to say hi. Bo tried to hug Ida Mae, and you know what she said?"

"I'm almost afraid to ask but go ahead," said Monique.

"She said, 'Back up off me, homie. I don't swing that way. I'm strictly dickly over here.' Bitch, I was on the floor dying laughing."

Wine spewed from Eve's mouth.

Monique smiled in an attempt to hide her embarrassment. "Let's change the subject, please."

"So, umm… Na'Tosha… Speaking of Bo…" Eve began asking.

"Bo came by, I didn't let her in. She begged, I declined. She called me a bitch. I called her P.O. No answer, so I left a voicemail. She asked for her PlayStation, I threw it out the window. She's probably on her way to jail. If not, that's fine too. As long as she stays far the fuck from around me. End of story. Let's move on now, please and thank you."

Eve wished she hadn't asked. "Sheesh."

"Yes, sheesh is right… So, Monique… When are you linking up with mister rose man? That's the real question."

"Yes, Mo. You need to make that happen A.S.A.P.," added Eve.

"I am. I am… I just pray that I don't regret it… My intuition still says no…"

"Then find you a better intuition. The fuck," screamed Na'Tosha.

"Well... I hate to change the subject buuutt... Tomorrow I'm dropping these damn kids off to they nothing-ass daddy." Eve raised her hands. "Yes, Lord. Won't He do it."

"Look at you. You ain't gon' know what to do with a free weekend," said Na'Tosha.

"I know what I'm not going to be doing. And that's playing referee to these kids, constantly wrestling, hopping, jumping, tattle-telling... 'Mommy, D.J. ate my pizza' knowing good and damn well she wasn't gon' finish it... 'Mommy, Denesha keeps messing with my video game' knowing good and damn well she wanna play too. See, it's okay when ya lil' nappy headed friends wanna play, but nooo, when ya lil' sister wanna play, it's a problem. I knew I shouldn't have bought that damn game in the first place. I paid three hundred dollars, and every time I turn around, somethings wrong with it." Eve sipped her wine and fanned herself. "Wheeeww. I'm sorry... Y'all forgive me. I had a little episode just now. I tend to get those from time to time. Whenever y'all have kids, trust me, you'll feel my pain."

Monique looked on in astonishment. "You make me want to get my tubes tied."

Na'Tosha refilled her glass. "Tied? Bitch g'on 'head and just rip mines the fuck out."

CHAPTER TEN

It was Eve's first time having a few days alone since the separation and Deshaun was picking up the kids. He'd promised to take the children for one week out of each month, but regularly made excuses not to do so. Sure, she could've leaned on her mom, Monique, or Na'Tosha for a quick break, but that wasn't her style. Eve didn't believe in putting her children off on other people unless it was absolutely necessary. She refused to be looked at as the type of mother who abused her support system. She fully understood the non-stop commitment of being a mother, and she embraced the task with all her heart. However, even the most dedicated parent needed an occasional day or two to themselves.

Eve and the kids waited in the Walmart parking lot located in Hawthorne, on Inglewood Avenue. It was 11:45 a.m., meaning Deshaun was already thirty minutes late. She could've just dropped them off to him on her way to get her nails done but he insisted on meeting in this spot. Eve repeatedly called his phone, only to receive the voicemail. Her frustration grew by the second. If Deshaun didn't show up, it wouldn't be the first time he fell short. Eve had grown accustomed to his perpetual inconsistencies.

The children, on the other hand, patiently waited in the backseat. D.J. rapped, word for word, to songs on the radio, while Denisha played games on her iPad. Both kids were neatly dressed and prepared for whatever activities Deshaun had planned for the day. Eve's attire was geared more towards comfort; she had on tights, a baggy sweatshirt, no make-up, and her hair was wrapped in a scarf.

Eve glanced at her watch again. "Come on, Deshaun... Where are you? I'm going to be late for my nail appointment."

Ten minutes later, Deshaun arrived, and he wasn't alone. Donna was comfortably seated in the passenger seat of his blue Cadillac Escalade.

Eve's initial thought was to get out and drag her across the lot. "I know he didn't bring this bitch with him."

The kids charged out of Eve's car, exuberated. They were always so excited to see their dad. At times, it bothered Eve because she was the one there day in and day out while Deshaun came and went as he saw fit.

Deshaun bent down to hug the kids. "What's up? I missed y'all."

"We missed you too, daddy," echoed both kids.

Deshaun and the kids competed in a dance off whenever greeting each other. He started it off with a dance move called the "milly rock."

"No, Dad it's like this," D.J. corrected his dad with a better version of the dance.

Deshaun and Denisha both cheered him on. "AYE. AYE. AYE. AYE."

"Step back, D.J. and watch a pro do it." Denesha pushed D.J. aside and bested them both.

Eve was upset with Deshaun for being late but couldn't contain her smile as she watched her babies show out.

That smile was quickly removed when Donna, feeling left out, uninvitingly chimed into the competition. She rolled down the driver side window and in a corny, dry, awkward way shouted, "Aye. Aye."

Eve desperately wanted to get out and strangle her but caught a sense of relief as she witnessed Deshaun, D.J. and Denisha blankly staring until Donna rolled the window up and nearly crumbed into her seat.

"Umm can y'all speed up this little dance competition? I have somewhere I need to be, and I'm already running late," said Eve before folding her arms and staring Deshaun down.

"Hey... Go tell y'all momma bye so we can roll out."

Both kids rushed into Deshaun's car, while unenthusiastically waving bye to Eve.

"See how y'all do me when y'all daddy come around? It's okay, tho'."

Deshaun smiled and leaned into Eve's window. "Does Daddy get a kiss goodbye?"

"Boy, please. Go ahead and get back over there to little Ms. Becky so I can make my nail appointment."

"Nail appointment? So, that's where my child support payments been going?"

Eve couldn't believe Deshaun's audacity. "Excuse me? I do have a job, you know? I mean... Am I not supposed to maintain myself?"

"That whack-ass bank job ain't nothing worth bragging about. All I'm saying is, just the other day you were complaining about the kid's tuition... Now you're going out, getting all pampered and shit."

"Look, I'm not about to do this with you today. I have to go." Eve attempted to roll up her window.

Deshaun firmly pressed his elbow against it and gave Eve an intimidating stare. "You know what? Yeah, you go ahead and get those nails done. I can see that it's long overdue, and while you're at it, you might want to do something about that scalp too. I see that natural look aint workin' out too well." Deshaun reached for Eve's hair.

"Don't fuckin' touch me," said Eve, as she slapped his hand down.

Deshaun raised both hands in a defensive manner. "Woah, woah, baby don't hurt me." He smiled with glory before arrogantly careening away. "Piece out, baby... I love you."

CHAPTER ELEVEN

Na'Tosha moseyed into her apartment complex with her cell phone pressed to her ear with Monique on the other end.

"Why am I so nervous?" asked Monique. *"It's not like I never dated Mario before."*

"Bitch, I don't know why but you need to get it together. A lil convo, some good food, and a couple drinks ain't never hurt nobody."

"You're right... A few drinks won't hurt."

Na'Tosha panted as she jogged up the stairs, leading to her second story apartment. *"I said a couple not a few, hoe. You know how yo' ass get off too much liquor."*

Monique laughed. *"Shut up. Anyways... Thanks for fitting me in on such short notice. I know Saturdays are your super busy days."*

"You're welcome... Besides, you need this date. You and yo' loneliness was starting to get on my damn nerves."

Monique smiled as she admired herself in the mirror. *"Why didn't you tell me my butt was getting bigger."*

"Girl, all them late night gym sessions got dat ass sittin' right," said Na'Tosha.

Monique wore a black off the shoulder, midi, body-con-styled dress. Even she couldn't help but be impressed by the way it wrapped around her body. Her shoe collection was amongst the best. It consisted of top designers from all over the globe. For this occasion, she went with her favorite, Coco Chanel. Earlier that day, Na'Tosha added honey-brown highlights and styled her hair into an asymmetrical bob. It was a little different from what she was accustomed to, but it went great with her cute almond-shaped face.

"This is him calling me on the other line. He must be outside, girl let me go."

"G'on 'head and let that bald, tall, sophisticated, bomb-ass man wine and dine you."

"Thanks, boo. Call you when it's over... Bye."

Na'Tosha placed the phone into her purse and located her keys. As she opened the door, a strong hand gripped her shoulder.

"Hey, baby," said Bo.

Na'Tosha flinched. "You just scared the shit out of me. What are you even doing here?"

"I'm here because I love you." Bo reached from behind and handed Na'Tosha a large gift bag.

Na'Tosha's eyes bulged and her mouth dropped once she realized what Bo revealed. "Wow, a Birken bag?"

Bo smiled after seeing Na'Tosha's facial expression. "It's the one that you've been stacking up for, right? Go ahead... Look inside."

Na'Tosha peeked into the high-end French leather bag and discovered an even bigger surprise. It was a rose-gold, day-date Rolex watch, with a twenty-pointer diamond bezel. "A Rolex, too?"

"Just a little something to show how much I care," said Bo.

As much as Na'Tosha wanted to keep the lavish gifts, something just didn't sit well. "Who'd you rob or finesse out of this? I hope you didn't do that shit before you came here?"

"I ain't rob nobody. Dang," said Bo.

"Here, I'm good... I can't take these."

Bo looked at Na'Tosha sideways. "What do you mean, you can't take them?"

"If I take these, you're going to think we still have a chance to be together, and truth is... Bo, I'm done. I can't take all the bullshit no more. I need to focus on my career and getting myself together. All this is too much."

Bo stared into Na'Tosha's eyes. "Baby, I know that I fucked up. You've always been there for me no matter what—when my mom died, when I got shot, jail stints, losses. When nobody else cared, you had my back. Truth is, when I lost you... I lost my soul. The thing that hurts most is that I can't blame anybody but myself. These gifts aren't about us getting back together. They're about me at least giving you something that you've been wanting, since I wasn't able to be the person that you've been needing—look, I'm going to get out of here. Please, keep the gifts—you deserve them." Bo handed Na'Tosha the bag and watch before slow dragging away.

"Bo," called out Na'Tosha.

"Yeah?" responded Bo before reaching the stairway.

"This was really sweet of you... Thanks."

"It ain't no thang... You're welcome, tho'." Bo had one last request as Na'Tosha turned to step foot into her apartment, "Can I ask you for a favor?"

"See, I knew it was a catch. Here, take this shit. I don't want it."

"Hold up. It ain't even like that... I have to piss. Can I use the bathroom?" asked Bo.

"Man, piss outside. You're just trying to get into my house."

Bo stared at Na'Tosha while pointing down towards her crotch.

Na'Tosha, against her better judgement, swung the door open to let Bo in. "Oh, yeah—that's right—come on, but you better hurry up. After you pee, yo' ass gotta go."

Bo happily skipped towards the door like a kid entering a candy store. She playfully smacked Na'Tosha on the butt and jogged backwards in the direction of the bathroom. "It's all good... Chill. I'm pissin' then I'm out."

It's Happened to the Best of Us

"My damn head hurt," mumbled Na'Tosha as she wiped morning crust from her eyes. After yawning and stretching, her senses kicked in. *Who's playing music this fuckin' early? And is that bacon I smell? Wait... Is that shit coming from my kitchen?* Na'Tosha jolted from the bed. She grabbed a metal Louisville Slugger baseball bat from underneath the bed and made her way towards the kitchen.

Clothes were scattered throughout the hallway and empty bottles of Hennessey Pure White were lying on the floor.

"What the fuck?" whispered Na'Tosha as she tried to make sense of what might've taken place, but nothing registered. She tip-toed into the kitchen with the bat cocked. What she saw next made her heart drop. Na'Tosha tossed the bat, fell to her knees, and cried, "No. No. No. Na'Tosha, nooo." It was at that very moment Na'Tosha realized she'd screwed up big time.

Bo was at the stove scrambling eggs. Her only clothing was an apron and oven mitt. She turned around and noticed Na'Tosha on her knees. Bo smiled, lifted the apron, and revealed a strap-on dildo with a condom on it. "I was gon' ask how many eggs you wanted, but it looks like you want some more of this sausage."

Na'Tosha had vowed to never allow Bo back into her life, and here Bo was in the kitchen, butt-naked, looking like Melvin from "Baby Boy." How could she allow this to happen? How could she let this person back into her life again? Was it love? Was it lust? Or, was it just an unhealthy pattern of dysfunction? Either way, it just wasn't right. The combination of embarrassment, disappointment, shame, and flat out stupidity was too much to handle. Na'Tosha fainted smack dab in the middle of the floor.

CHAPTER TWELVE

It was the grand opening of Morton's Steakhouse, located in the heart of Beverly Hills. Monique and Mario sat across from one another at a dimly lit table. The sound of soft piano-themed music filled the air, as the two finished up mouthwatering Wagyu Beef, lobster mac and cheese, and parmesan encrusted a-sparagus.

Mario appeared even more handsome to Monique than their last encounter. She was on her third glass of wine and could've easily attributed his good looks to that. However, she couldn't deny the warm, tingly feeling his deep, raspy voice gave her. Being 6'7" didn't hurt him either. Muscles from his arms and chest bulged through his royal blue, Italian blazer and Mario's peanut butter complexion meshed well with his clean-shaven head and perfectly trimmed goatee. He was serving serious Boris Kodjoe vibes.

Monique sat across from Mario, the youngest Senior Account Executive for the third largest solar company in the United States. His master's degree in marketing doubled as an extra incentive. This man was the perfect combination of business and pleasure. How could a man so well rounded be so available? Monique had that question and a few others that needed answers.

Apparently, Mario had his own questions. "So... Can we finally address the elephant in the room?"

"Elephant?" Monique looked around the room and smiled. "I haven't seen one in here... Have you?"

"You're something else, Monique."

"I'm sure I can be at times."

Mario stared deeply into her eyes. "Let's just cut to the chase... Why haven't you called me? I thought that things were going really well between us."

Monique fidgeted with her fork. "Yeah... Well, I've been extremely busy. Work has been demanding and mentally draining, to say the least. I was going to reach out to you..."

"Is that so?"

"Yeah... Eventually."

A waiter approached the table. "Was everything to your satisfaction?"

Monique reached into her purse. "Everything was great. Thanks... Can we have the check, please?"

"Most certainly, ma'am... Take your time." The waiter placed the check on the table before taking off.

"What are you doing?" asked Mario.

"I'm paying for dinner... That's the least I can do to thank you for the beautiful roses you sent me."

"Absolutely not. You'll never pay for a thing as long as I'm around."

Although flattered, Monique kindly disagreed, "That's sweet and all, buuut—I'm a strong, independent black woman, and I do pretty well for myself. I don't mind picking up the tab—from time to time."

Mario gently grabbed Monique's hands and caressed them with his thumbs. "Monique Lynnette Harris. Can I tell you something?"

Her panties moistened from his strong, yet tender grip. "Sure... Go ahead."

"I want you. And I'm going to have you. The sooner you realize that, the better off you'll be. I'm going to treat you better than you could ever imagine any man treating you. You stimulate my mind—your very presence exudes sex appeal. Your ambition, class, grace, and strength are impeccable attributes. I'm not easily impressed, but you've made an unforgettable impression on me. And the fact of the matter is my persistence won't waver until I have the privilege of calling you mine."

Mario's words stimulated Monique's mind. Chills raced down her spine as his juicy lips uttered this bold proclamation.

Monique's turn-on meter was at one hundred. Yet, she managed to play it cool. "Hmmm... Is that so?"

Mario gazed without blinking. "Very much so."

"Is that what you tell all the ladies?"

"Not at all. I've never met a woman worthy of me saying it to—until now."

"Interesting," said Monique.

"How so?"

"Well, I just find it hard to believe that a handsome and accomplished man of your stature has a hard time meeting nice, well-rounded women."

"I never said it was hard," said Mario.

"Oh... Well, excuse me."

Mario moved in closer. "It's like this... I know exactly what I want. And I'm a man of strong will. Not only do I set out to accomplish—I set out to SMASH any and every obstacle that might prevent me from doing so."

Mario had Monique's undivided attention. It had been a long time since she felt these vibes, and he was saying all the right things.

"Did you just say, smash?" asked Monique.

Mario eased over closer. Their chairs were now side by side. He softly placed two fingers onto Monique's chin and gently brushed his beard against her cheek. Then, he took the tip of his tongue and delicately grazed the bottom of Monique's ear.

Shock waves rushed throughout her body.

Next, he whispered in the strongest, deepest, seductive tone his voice could muster, "SMAAAASSHH, baby—I didn't stutter."

After a short ride from the restaurant, the two landed in front of Monique's place. The sexual tension between them was insurmountable. It'd been well over a year since Monique had had sex. Needless to say, the cookie was well baked and in dire need of being gobbled up.

Monique's conscience played tricks on her the whole ride home. The right side of her mind said, not just yet, hold out. But, the left side of her mind, where all the alcohol was stored, said, g'on 'head and get you some, girl. You deserve it. Monique prided herself on being a classy, responsible, intelligent woman with morals. Although under the influence, her decision would ultimately be the one that properly suited her best.

Mario politely escorted Monique to the door and this gentlemanly gesture further complicated Monique's dilemma. He reached in for a hug, wrapping his huge forearms around her delicate body. Monique closed her eyes and deeply inhaled the fresh scent of Mario's "1 Million" cologne. Its bold vapors entered her nostrils and navigated their way to her g-spot.

Monique grabbed Mario's wrist and directed his hands towards her ass. He squeezed her soft, plump cheeks, sending a euphoric sensation throughout her entire body. Mario bent down to meet Monique at eye level. He softly kissed her lips while rubbing his hands up and down her backside. Monique's body trembled under the raw strength of Mario's touch and reacted by reaching for his crotch.

Monique methodically massaged Mario's full erection. Her tight, wet honey hole gushed as his massive penis gyrated in her hand. Monique opened the front door with one hand but firmly latched onto the dick with the other. She slowly led Mario towards the couch and pushed him onto it. She lifted her dress waist-high before straddling Mario on the sofa. Suddenly, her conscience kicked in.

"Should we really be doing this so soon?"

"I don't know, but I'll stop if you want me to," replied Mario.

Monique tried her best to make a rational decision, but her thoughts were impaired. Not necessarily from the wine, but from the undeniably lustful energy between the two. Her mind was telling her no, but her body had other ideas.

Monique bit her bottom lip and stared into Mario's eyes. "Nah—keep going."

Mario felt his shaft grow at the sound of Monique's desire to continue. He'd envisioned this moment for a while and had every intension on rightfully seizing it. Mario lifted Monique's dress over her head and tossed it across the room. He slowly licked around her succulent breasts, occasionally grazing the nipples with each motion of his tongue, making her moan and tremble in ecstasy. Mario was just getting started. He grabbed Monique's waist and in one motion, propelled her on to his face. The warmth of her forbidden fruit heated his tongue while he licked, nibbled, and gently sucked piece by piece.

Monique rode his face like a champion bull rider. Her body motioned in sensual circles as she grinded her clit against his oral apparatus. Monique reached back and unzipped Mario's pants. She carefully massaged his balls, sending his body into a complete frenzy. Mario became so hard that thick veins protruded throughout his third leg. Monique flipped herself around and positioned into the sixty-nine. She sloppily spit and massaged his stick, teasing Mario as her juicy throat gradually took in as much of him as it could. Monique took her time rubbing his pipe with both hands, in opposite directions, like grinding pepper. She felt his body tense up. The brute strength from his hardened frame turned Monique on even more. Her ass uncontrollably bounced up and down on Mario's face as he spelled his name across her pussy.

They were completely at each other's mercy. Mario fought back moans as his toes curled. He strategically licked from the top of Monique's sweet spot down towards her grocery department. She was wetter than the Pacific Ocean. Her sugar glazed over Mario's beard like a Krispy Kreme donut.

Monique licked his shaft like her life depended on it. She occasionally sucked his balls while quickly stroking the head of his snake.

Mario felt himself about to explode but he had a point to prove, so he fought back his nut for as long as he could. He positioned one leg from the couch onto the floor. In an act of absolute dominance, he swiveled around, stood to his feet, and flung Monique over his shoulder. Mario carried her into the kitchen and cleared off the entire counter with one swipe of his arm. Monique sprung off of his shoulder onto the surface. She laid her chest flat against the granite and tooted her ass with her back in a perfect arch. Mario grabbed both of Monique's arms while aiming his rock-hard strap into her love box.

Monique gasped as he entered her confined space. Her tight, wet pussy pulsated with each stroke when Mario randomly switched the pace, alternating slow, deep, sensual, grinding strokes with fast, long, powerful, pounding thrust. Monique went from loudly moaning Mario's name, to calling out for Jesus in a matter of pumps. Her legs twitched as her river came flowing down his water slide.

Mario released an arm and hooked his hand underneath Monique's chin. His face grimaced as he let out a deep groan. He pulled out and released his secretion all over Monique's backside. The two breathed heavily as sweat dripped from both their bodies.

Monique scooted away from the counter but lost her balance as she tried to gather.

Mario caught her before she hit the ground.

"Oh my, gosh... My legs are like noodles," said Monique.

Mario looked down towards his own noodle and joked. "Thank him, not me."

The two laughed while exiting the kitchen. Monique was on cloud nine. And to think, she wasn't even going to call the man back.

CHAPTER THIRTEEN

Eve and Monique were seated on the patio area of a local restaurant known as The Pan. The small, quaint diner was famous for its signature loaded hash browns and pineapple pancakes. The Pan had been a mainstay in the ladies' lives since high school. No one loved eating there more than Na'Tosha. So, her tardiness for this occasion was abnormal. Although she was notorious for being late, the rare times that she did show up on schedule were all food related.

A waitress approached the table with two glasses of water. "Have you ladies had time to go over the menu?"

Monique grinned from ear to ear, having the energy of a woman who'd just won the lottery. "Not yet, hun. We're still waiting for our friend, but we'll be sure to let you know as soon as we're ready."

Eve turned in Monique's direction with one eyebrow raised. Something was odd about her demeanor.

"Okay, no problem... I'll come back in a few minutes."

Monique smiled and affectionately tapped the waitress's arm. "Thanks, sweetie."

"You're welcome."

Monique turned towards Eve. "Isn't it such a beautiful day? The sun is out, people walking, talking, and just doing regular stuff..."

"Umm, Mo... You seem a little extra this morning," said Eve.

"Who, me? Nooo."

Eve locked eyes with Monique and took a sip of water. "Yes, you."

Na'Tosha crept in shortly after, disguised in a fedora, oversized shades, and a full-length trench coat. She sat at the table, looking in all directions.

Eve's suspicion unexpectedly had a new target. "Bitch, why are you walking in here looking like where in the world is Carmen San Diego? And is that a new bag I see?" Eve reached across the table and analyzed Na'Tosha's new prize. She quickly noticed that there was more than one. "And a new rollie? Oh, you ballin' ballin', huh?"

Na'Tosha yanked her purse from Eve's grasp. "Ha-ha... You got jokes. These are old. I bought them off the street. They're not even real." Na'Tosha fake coughed. "Oh, and this coat is because—umm—I think I'm coming down with something."

Eve wasn't buying Na'Tosha being sick.

Monique, on the other hand, was in la-la land. The only thing she heard from the conversation was Carmen San Diego. Monique closed her eyes, snapped her fingers, and sang her own ratchet rendition of the early 90s kid's show theme song, "Where in the world is, Carmen San Diego. Tell me where in the world is, Carmen San Diego. Tell me..."

Eve wasn't in the mood. "Mo, okay, okay. We get it."

Monique opened her eyes and noticed everyone on the patio staring at her. "Oops—my bad."

Eve looked back and forth between Monique and Na'Tosha. They'd been her best friends for more than half of her life. It didn't take much for her to realize that something was unusual. "You know what? You two heffas are acting real suspect right about now. Mo, first yo' mean ass come in here acting all extra friendly with the waitress, now you over here singing and dancing to a damn show that hasn't been on in twenty years. Then here come Ms. Incognito, bringing her ass in here late, all bundled up in eighty-five-degree weather, faking like she has a damn cold, brand new Rolex watch and a fresh Birkin bag?"

Eve stopped her tirade and noticed that Monique was too busy handing out compliments to a young lady seated next to her.

"Girl, your nails are so cute. That's a pretty color. And your hair..." Monique felt Eve and Na'Tosha staring at her. "What? I can't be nice? I'm just fixing another queen's crown. Dang."

"Whatever. I can't with y'all. Let's just order this food," said Eve.

Na'Tosha pushed her menu aside. "I'm not hungry. I already ate."

Eve rubbed her face in exasperation. "You've been talking about coming here all week long, and all of a sudden, you're telling me that you ate already?"

Na'Tosha timidly grabbed the menu and buried her head in it.

"Mo, do you hear this? We've been here waiting on this wench all this time, and she done already ate."

Monique didn't hear a word. She was in deep thought, drifting off into the sky, smiling at two birds chasing one another in the clouds.

"Mo—Mo—Mo!" Eve slapped the table causing Monique and Na'Tosha to jump.

Monique, unmindful to what was taking place, agreed with Eve. "Yeah, yeah girl you're right."

Suddenly, Eve said while aiming her butter knife, "Hold up. Hold up—wait an effin' freaking minute—"

Na'Tosha cut her off with a look of indictment, "—Why you gotta say freakin'... Wasn't nobody freakin'."

"You nasty little heffas. It's only two things that could make y'all act like this." She pointed at Monique. "New, good dick..." And then at Na'Tosha. "And old, guilty dick."

Monique stuck her tongue out and waved her hand.

Na'Tosha dropped her head on the table and broke down crying hysterically.

"Okay. Okay. All right—I confess." Na'Tosha removed her hat, shades, and jacket, revealing an enormous, hideous hickey across the right side of her neck. "So, Bo came by..."

"Bo came by?" asked Eve with an attitude.

"Yes, but it wasn't even like that."

Eve objected, "What was it like then, Na'Tosha?"

Na'Tosha sulked as she explained her position, "I was unlocking my door and out of nowhere—there she was with a Birkin bag in her hand, with a new watch inside. Next thing you know, she's telling me all this sweet stuff that I never heard her say before."

"Then you just gave it up," yelled Eve."

"No, she asked to use the bathroom."

"You should've told her to pee outside," said Monique.

"I did but..." Na'Tosha pointed between her legs.

"She hasn't figured out how to do that yet?" asked Monique.

Na'Tosha rolled her eyes. "Anyways—I woke up this morning, head throbbin', coochie throbbin', Hennessy bottles all over the floor. I went into the kitchen and Bo was standing there butt-ass naked cooking eggs."

"It was at that moment you knew you f'd up," said Monique in the All-State man's voice.

"Shut up. That ain't funny," said Na'Tosha.

Eve nodded her head in disappointment. "Mmm—mmm—mmm."

"So, basically you ate the eggs and the sausage—I mean eggplant." Monique leaned over and whispered in Eve's ear, "Or whatever they like to call they plastic junk."

Na'Tosha pouted. "I did and that's why I'm not hungry no more."

"And you had the nerve to tell me not to give my cookies up last night," said Monique.

Eve lashed out at Monique, "No, you didn't."

"What? Bitch, please. I'm grown—and I'm not sorry about that, or the curse word I just used."

Eve laughed. "Well, I take it you had a good night?"

"Good?" Monique snapped her fingers and arched her back. "Try great."

"Great, huh? Details please?" asked Eve.

Monique's eyes lit up as she recapped her remarkable night with Mario. "So, we went to this beautiful restaurant in Beverly Hills, we ate, had drinks—"

"—Had sex," Na'Tosha interrupted.

"No, smart ass. For your information, we fuc—"

The waitress appeared. "—I'm sorry to interrupt, but are you ladies ready to order now?"

Monique already had a meal in mind. "Yes, I'll have the..."

Eve swiftly put her finger up, causing Monique to pause. "Thanks, but we need a few more minutes."

"Sure thing—I'll be back shortly." The waitress pocketed her order pad and proceeded to another table.

"Too bad you didn't get none last night, lil' miss feisty ass," said Na'Tosha.

Eve gave her the middle finger while looking at Monique. "Mo, please continue."

Monique felt warm and fuzzy just thinking about Mario. A huge smile graced her face. "He walked me to the door and stared into my eyes. His cologne smelled so good. I tried to keep my composure, but I just couldn't. He even tried to be a gentleman and resist. But I was like, nah bruh, you about to get this work."

"Just plain ole nasty," said Na'Tosha.

Eve gave her the side eye. "I know you're not talking."

Na'Tosha slouched into her chair. "Let me get back to this menu that I'm not finna order from."

"Yeah, you do that," yelled Eve.

Monique fanned herself as she reminisced about last night's rendezvous, "Next thing I know, I'm on the kitchen counter, bent up like a pretzel, getting my back blew out."

Eve smirked. "And to think, you wasn't even going to call the man back."

Na'Tosha clapped her hands. "Crazy how the Lord work, ain't it?"

Monique pointed to the sky. "Yes, indeed. Yes, indeed."

"Both y'all skanks nasty," Eve paused and stuck out her bottom lip. "I'm jealous."

"For what tho'? You could be gettin' that 'Love and Basketball' wood from coach, what's-his-name, but you the one playing," said Na'Tosha.

"First off, I was referring to Mo's situation. You know—the one with an accomplished MAN. Who's got his ish together. Ain't nobody jealous of your little back and forth Jerry Springer ordeal with crusty, two, three timing-ass Bo."

Na'Tosha leaned back in her seat. "Why do you keep coming fa me? You've been on my head ever since I got here. Look, I had a moment with someone that I was with for almost five years. You're acting like I slept with some random."

"It doesn't matter. You keep doubling back expecting different, knowing good and damn well that nothing's going to change."

Na'Tosha fired back. "Kind of how you did with Deshaun, huh?"

Monique tried to intervene. "Hey, Na'Tosha—don't go there."

"Nah, fuck that. Eve, you have a lot of damn nerve telling me about a double back when you let the same good-for-nothing-ass MAN dog you for years."

Eve rose from her seat. "That was my husband. We exchanged vows. 'Til death do us part. Something your ghetto, confused, ratchet ass will never know about."

Monique stood between the two as tempers flared. "Okay. Now y'all are going too far. Just calm down. It's bad enough we're already causing a scene."

Na'Tosha grabbed her things, stood, and calmly slid her chair underneath the table.

"Confused, huh? That was low but okay—since we're going there, you know what I'm not confused about? That school tuition that isn't paid for. Yeah, I saw that paper on yo' counter the other night—how about you focus more on that. I'm out, Mo. I'll call you later." Na'Tosha rushed out of the restaurant with her head held high and zero regret.

CHAPTER FOURTEEN

Eve tossed and turned as the sounds of heavy rain and lightning pounded against her window. Gloomy weather brought back memories of pain, humiliation, and torment. The recollection of Deshaun's deceit haunted Eve's dreams and made sleeping through a storm nearly impossible. Na'Tosha's comments struck her deeply. It seemed as if every time the wounds of divorce began to heal, a situation occurred and turned Eve's emotional clock backwards. To make matters worse, the school tuition still needed to be paid.

Eve really needed to get some sleep. She rolled over to set her alarm for an additional hour, only to realize that she was already thirty minutes behind schedule. She wanted to cry so badly but knew that it wouldn't change anything. She hopped up, wiped away the tear that managed to creep through, and shook back into mommy mode.

Eve went to wake up the kids, but heard noises coming from the living room. To her surprise, they were already dressed, eating breakfast, and watching cartoons. Denisha ran to her mother and hugged her tightly.

"Good morning, Mommy. How'd you sleep?"

Eve lied, "Good baby, and you?"

"I slept really good. Mommy, look. D.J. cooked breakfast and ironed my uniform."

"Oh, is that so? Did he burn the house down too?"

D.J. gallantly smiled as he embraced his mother. "Good morning, Mommy. Are you hungry? I made oatmeal and scrambled eggs, just the way you taught me."

"Aww. Thanks, but no, baby. I'm fine. Mommy doesn't have an appetite this morning. You're such a handsome little helper. I'm so proud of you."

"Little?"

Eve chuckled. "Young helper—excuse me, sir. My apologies."

D.J. smiled and squeezed Eve's waist tightly. "That's more like it."

Eve bent down and kissed his cheek. She didn't have to bend too far though. D.J. took on his dad's height. He was the tallest and most athletic nine-year old in his school. His future in sports was bright, although academics were top priority in Eve's household. It seemed like just yesterday she was changing his dirty diapers. Now D.J. was old enough to iron and cook breakfast.

Denisha was growing up as well. The athletic gene hadn't skipped her either. She proudly bragged about being the fastest kid in her class. Eve found it adorable that Denisha accredited this accolade to a particular pair of old shoes, which she refused to get rid of.

Eve was in love with the bond that her children were developing with each other. Of course, they bickered, but at the end of the day, they had each other's back. That's all a mother could ask for. The kids were her motivation, and times like these, were when she needed it most.

Eve looked at the clock. They were now thirty-five minutes behind and needed to get a step on it. "Okay guys, come on. It's time to get a move on it. We're already running late."

D.J. looked at his mom's panicked face. "Umm, Mom?"

"Yes, handsome?"

"We're dressed already. You're the one still in your pajamas."

Both kids laughed as Eve looked down at her clothes.

Eve grinned before rushing towards the bathroom. "Honey, you're right—I'll be ready in five minutes."

Denisha rolled her eyes at D.J. "Okay, Mommy." She leaned over and whispered to her brother, "That really means ten."

D.J. whispered back, "Yeah, right—fifteen if we're lucky."

"I heard that," shouted Eve from the back of the apartment.

"How does she do that?" asked D.J.

"I don't know. I think she knows magic," replied Denisha.

The three were now at the entrance of St. Joseph's Preparatory Academy. Both kids rushed towards their classrooms with tardy notes in hand. Eve blew them kisses as they scurried off.

Principle Clarkson was patrolling the hallway as usual and approached Eve with an envelope. "Good morning, Evelyn."

"Good morning, Mrs. Clarkson. I was under the impression that I had a little more time to get the payment to you."

"Oh no, darling. That's your receipt."

"Receipt?"

"The children's tuition was paid in full this morning. Were you not aware of it?"

"Uh—yeah—sure, I was. I just didn't know that he was going to pay it today. Their dad can be full of surprises, ya know." Eve chuckled in a perplexed state.

"But it wasn't their father who made the payment," said Principal Clarkson.

Eve was confused. "Huh? Then who was it?"

"It was a woman by the name of Ms. Monique Harris, if I'm not mistaken. She dropped by this morning, stated that she was the kids' Godmother and wanted to pay the balance for the remainder of the school year."

Eve was embarrassed. "Oh, did she? Well, thanks for letting me know, Mrs. Clarkson." She pretended to check her watch. "I'm running late for work and I have to get going—have a wonderful day."

"Thanks, and same to you."

Eve stormed out of the school with mixed emotions. She appreciated Monique's gesture, but didn't understand why she would do it without notifying her first. Since Eve's separation, Monique had done a number of financial deeds. Some were out of the kindness of her heart. Others were done out of guilt from an incident that occurred a few years prior. She knew that Monique wasn't aware of Eve's knowledge regarding the incident, and really didn't know how to tell her. Eve did her best to forgive and let go, but certain situations only refreshed the feelings of betrayal.

Needless to say, Eve was overwhelmed, and it wasn't even 9 a.m. Using a sick day didn't seem like such a bad idea. She called her boss and told him she wouldn't be able to make it in. Eve wasn't physically ill, but a mental health day was an appropriate excuse. The plan was to catch up on some rest until it was time to grab the kids from school. But before she could relax, there was something Eve needed to get off her chest.

CHAPTER FIFTEEN

Na'Tosha barely managed to tumble into her apartment, balancing groceries stacked higher than she could see. Her legs ached from carrying the extra weight up two long flights of stairs. She opened the door to find that Bo's trifling ass had been in the apartment the whole time. Na'Tosha gagged at the sight of Bo slouched on the couch in a tank-top, boxers, and only one sock. The place was a complete mess with dirty dishes covering the coffee table and blunt guts and ashes toppled the area rug.

Bo yelled into a video game headset as she concentrated on a game of Fortnite.

Out of breath, and understandably frustrated, Na'Tosha dropped the bags onto the living room floor.

"Bo, you didn't see me calling yo' phone?"

Bo looked at her phone, revealing several missed calls from Na'Tosha. "Nah baby, I ain't get no missed call. How was work, tho'?"

Na'Tosha sucked her teeth and rolled her eyes. "It was work. Question is, what have you been doing all day?"

"Shit—chillin'," replied Bo.

"Umm, can you pause that game for a second?"

"Yeah, hold up, baby. Give me a couple more minutes."

Na'Tosha smacked her lips, grabbed a few bags, and stumped into the kitchen with an attitude.

"What the fuck? This house is a got-damn mess. Why is it so hard for you to clean up after yourself?"

Bo's eyes never budged from the television screen. "My bad, baby. I was going to cleanup, but shit—now you're here—I know you got it under control."

"Excuse me?"

Bo turned off the video game, picked up her phone, and replied to an incoming text. "Hey, baby? I need to use your car for a couple of hours. I have a few moves to make."

"No, the fuck you don't. The last time I let you use my car, you got a parking ticket and didn't put gas in it. On top of that, you brought it back smelling like ass."

Bo snuck up on Na'Tosha and forced herself upon her. "Come on, baby. Don't be like that. I'm going to pay the ticket, you know that. I'll only be gone a few hours."

"A few hours? You said a couple, not a few."

Bo smiled. "A couple of hours—my bad."

Na'Tosha closed her eyes as Bo softly kissed her neck. "I swear, you better not have no gang bangers, or stank-ass hoes in my car, Bo."

"Baby, I'm not. I just have a few things that I need to do real quick."

"I swear yo' ass make me sick." Na'Tosha pushed Bo off and handed over the keys. "Here."

Bo cheesed from ear to ear. "Thanks, baby."

"Yeah, yeah whateva—I'm not playing about my car, Bo."

Bo quickly threw on her clothes. "Damn, all right, I heard you—what do you want to eat tonight?"

Now Bo was talking Na'Tosha's language. It's amazing how just the idea of food turned her frown upside down. "Oh, snap. Let me see—lately, I've been craving that sweet and sour pork from Kim's off of Western."

Bo licked her lips. "That sounds so good right about now."

"Oh, get some beef and broccoli, too. And extra sweet and sour sauce, please."

"Okay, baby. I got you—see, you don't even have to cook tonight."

Na'Tosha turned the water on in the sink, squirting dish detergent, and dropped a cap of bleach over the pile of dirty dishes.

Bo crept up behind Na'Tosha again and softly caressed one of her breasts. "Hey, bae? Give me like fifty bucks. I'll give it to you when I get back."

"Are you serious?"

"Chill baby, I'll give it right back to you tonight."

Na'Tosha slammed a fork into the sink. "Ugghh, go get it out of my purse. I want my money back, too. Shit."

"Thanks, bae." Bo tried to put her hand down Na'Tosha's pants.

"Bye, Bo. Hurry up before I change my mind."

Bo rushed out of the kitchen, in route to Na'Tosha's purse. She grabbed the money and hurried towards the front door.

"Aye baby, I took a hundred."

This time, Na'Tosha slammed a cup into the sink and went after Bo. "No, you said fifty. Give me my damn money, Bo."

Bo taunted Na'Tosha by licking her tongue out. She jetted out of the house with Na'Tosha's flying slipper narrowly missing her.

Na'Tosha looked around at the mess that Bo created. She'd been on her feet doing hair for ten hours, just to have to come home and do more work. Something had to give. This never-ending cycle was all too familiar. But Bo wasn't the only one at fault. It took two to tango, and Na'Tosha knew she was voluntarily dancing with the devil.

CHAPTER SIXTEEN

Monique sat at her desk and took a long sip from her morning coffee. Caffeine had become her Superman over the years. The day would be filled with countless e-mails to read and respond to, followed by consecutive meetings so her favorite cup of Joe would definitely become vital.

Monique's grind was rigorous. She was determined to earn another promotion by the end of the year. In order to do so, her work would have to be flawless. It was no secret that Monique was the homerun hitter of the firm. Nonetheless, her accomplishments were frequently overshadowed in a male-dominated field. It was practically unheard of for an African American female to climb the corporate ladder as quickly as Monique had. She was built for such challenges. The unfortunate circumstances growing up, fully prepared her for any obstacle that corporate America could dish out.

Growing up without a mother or father in South Central Los Angeles had its difficulties and forced her to become tougher than most. Over the years, she learned how to twist this ill-fate into an advantage. What was once viewed as a character flaw, coincidentally, became beneficial in the long run. Monique developed a "pit-bull in a skirt" mentality that helped her excel through grad school and transition perfectly into the world of Stockbroking.

After taking another sip from her mug, Monique heard Rebecca's familiar knock at the door. She took in a deep breath, letting it out slowly. "Yes. Come in, Rebecca."

Rebecca was dressed in a thigh-high mini skirt with a see through blouse that revealed more than Monique would've liked to see.

It must be time to give Mr. Froth his weekly dose of "medicine," Monique thought.

"Ms. Harris, there's a woman here to see you," said Rebecca.

"Does she have an appointment?"

"Actually, she doesn't. But from the look in her eyes, I think that it's urgent."

Monique glanced at her desk clock. "Okay—sure—send her in."

Rebecca gave Monique a huge, phony smile. "Yes, ma'am. Will do."

Eve barged through the door.

"Hey, girl. What's up?" asked Monique. "Aren't you supposed to be at work right now?"

Eve's face was as stiff as concrete. She rushed towards Monique and slammed the school tuition receipt onto her desk.

Monique picked it up and glanced over it. "Oh yeah, I meant to text you. I swung by on my way to work and took care of that for you. Don't worry. It's no big deal."

"Mo, it is a big deal. I don't need you running to my rescue every time you think I have a money issue."

"Whoa—okay, hold up a minute. Na'Tosha mentioned something about the kids' tuition at brunch while you both were arguing, so I figured I'd—"

Eve erupted, "—I don't give a damn what Na'Tosha said. I'm their mother. I got this shit under control."

"Eve, please, calm down. I was just trying to help."

"Yeah, I know. The same way you were just trying to help when you knew Deshaun was fucking Grandmommy's nurse and didn't say anything?"

"Eve..."

"The same damn way you were just trying to help when you found out he got her pregnant, too, right?"

Monique's eyes grew large. "I didn't know until it was already done. Once I found out, I immediately fired her. Before I came to you, I wanted to make sure that it was one hundred percent true. I didn't want to bring any more conflict to you and the kids. You were already going through so much."

Eve's tears streamed like an endless waterfall. "She carried his child and you kept it from me. You didn't say one single damn word to me about it. If it wasn't for Na'Tosha's messy ass I would've never known."

"I'm so sorry. I was just trying to protect you—I didn't want to make a bad situation worse."

Monique treaded over with caution and placed her hand on Eve's shoulder, but Eve pulled away.

"You know what, Monique? Don't even worry about it. I promise you, I'm going to pay you back every dime of that tuition money."

"I don't want the money back. I'm so sorry. I really am."

Eve wiped her tears, smoothed the wrinkles in her skirt before heading towards the door. "From here on out, I'd appreciate if you and Na'Tosha would fall the fuck back and let me worry about my own. I don't need anyone's charity or guilt offerings. Me and mine will be just fine."

Monique's voice wavered, "Yes, of course. As you wish."

The dilemma between seeing her best friend's feelings crushed and harboring detrimental information in an attempt to protect her, served as more of a daunting task than originally expected. Shielding Eve from additional sorrow seemed to only backfire in the end.

For years, Monique helplessly watched as the multitude of Deshaun's havoc spread vastly throughout Eve's realm. She knew there wasn't anything that she could do to fix the issue. In fact, taking it upon herself to clean things up is what landed the two there in the first place. The cat was now out of the bag and there was no turning back.

CHAPTER SEVENTEEN

The holidays were approaching and pressure of providing an adequate Christmas for her children tacked additional stress onto Eve's already full pallet of problems. Her finances were still an issue, Deshaun continued to be a thorn in her side, and she hadn't seen or spoken to neither of her besties in several weeks. The year couldn't end soon enough for her.

Na'Tosha's cosmetology business was thriving and at an all-time high. Her reputation as one of the top hairstylists in Southern California increased drastically after being introduced to a top executive for BET. This led to her doing work for the likes of Beyoncé, Cardi B, Meagan Thee Stallion, Nicki Minaj, and Rihanna. Women from all over the country booked appointments weeks in advance. But like a true friend, Na'Tosha made sure that Monique's monthly touch up remained a priority. Even though things were going well, she still hadn't figured out how to keep Bo out of her house—or her pockets.

Monique was just happy to finally have something outside of work keeping her busy. That something—or someone, for that matter was Mario. The two had been spending some serious time together. Things were now exclusive between them, and both were excited to spend their first holiday season together.

Monique and Mario strolled alongside the beautiful confines of Venice beach. Los Angeles was one of the few places in the U.S. where you could enjoy the ocean in December without freezing. The two held hands and shared an ice cream cone.

Monique was unusually quiet as her eyes ventured into the vibrant blue sky.

"Baby, is everything all right?" asked Mario. You seem as if something's bothering you."

"Yeah, but I'm fine. Thanks."

"Are you sure? You haven't quite been yourself today. And obviously, this ice cream isn't doing the trick like I thought it would." Mario smiled. Typically, his charm easily penetrated Monique's tough exterior. But whatever she was dealing with would require more persuasion.

"I'm good—trust me, I'm good."

Mario stopped and turned towards Monique. He stared deeply into her eyes, bearing his concern. "Monique, I care about you, and I'm going to be here for you through good and bad. But sweetheart, I can't help you if you don't let me in."

Monique could tell that Mario's intentions were sincere. Over the past six months he'd proven that. It was just difficult to let down a guard that she'd been holding up her entire life. The less people knew, the less they could judge.

"Thanks... That was sweet, but I don't need any help. I got it."

"Monique. Talk to me... Please... Let me carry some of this burden for you."

Mario's stern, but caring tone gave Monique a sense of comfort, speaking with so much conviction. Monique was falling for him more and more each day. She grabbed Mario's hand and they continued strolling along the boardwalk.

Monique took a deep breath. "Okay. So, there are a couple of things weighing heavy on my mind."

"Like?" asked Mario.

Monique sighed as she fought back tears. "My grandmother is really, really sick. If anything ever happened to her, I don't know what I'd do. My parents died in a car accident when I was three, so she raised me. She's really all I got left."

Mario hugged Monique tightly. Outside of sympathizing with her, he was fascinated by the fact that she'd withheld it for so long. This made him want to be there for her even more. "Baby, the passing of a loved one is never an easy thing to deal with... With that being said, death is the only thing that we're promised on this earth. It seems to me as if your grandma has lived a long, complete life. And, with the grace of God, I pray that she lives an even longer one. But, when it's her time to go, she'll leave proudly knowing that she raised a strong, intelligent, phenomenal young woman who's more than qualified to conquer the world."

Monique stopped and turned to Mario and buried her head into his chest. "You always know exactly what to say to make me smile."

"Making you smile is okay... But keeping you smiling is my ultimate goal."

Monique smiled and kissed him.

"So, you said you had a couple of things on your mind? Understandably the one that we just touched on was most important, but I'm curious to know what the other issue is."

"Look at you, trying to dig out all my problems... Are you turning into Dr. Phil on me now?"

Mario chuckled. "Not at all. I just want to be your stress reliever."

"Well... If you really want to help me relieve some stress..." Monique rubbed her hand against Mario's crotch. "You know exactly how to do that."

"That much I do know."

"On a serious note... I had a fall out with Eve and she's pretty upset with me right now."

"What happened?"

"So, Eve's ex-husband was a scumbag. Lying, cheating, the whole nine yards. One time in particular, he decided to spring himself on my grandmother's in-home care nurse."

"Ouch," said Mario.

"Yeah, that part... One night I stopped by to check on Grandmommy and noticed her nurse leaving... Guess whose car she was hopping into?"

"Eve's husband?"

"Bingo... At the time, I'm watching my friend who's completely torn apart over all the other things he'd been putting her through, as well as trying to juggle two kids, and I—"

"—Decided not tell her," replied Mario.

"Yes... I decided not to tell her. I wasn't trying to keep it from her... I just wanted to protect her feelings. I care about her and those babies so much."

"Well, did you tell her eventually?"

Monique sighed. "So, that's where things get tricky. I confronted the nurse and told her that Deshaun was a married man with children. I also mentioned that if she wanted to keep her license, it'd be wise for her to end their little fling, because I knew people in high places and I wouldn't have one problem cutting her faucet the fuck off. Sorry... Excuse my language."

Mario laughed. "Damn, like that?"

"Just like that. Don't play—she tells me that she's so sorry, how they'd just met, she didn't know he was married, that she's not a home wrecker, and she's going to cut it off right away... blah, blah, blah."

"Well, did she?"

"No, and me being so naïve... I gave the little skank the benefit of the doubt. A few months passed by, and guess what?"

"What?" asked Mario.

"Nurse Davis popped up with a baby bump. And take a wild guess who she claimed the pappy was?"

"I'm almost afraid to say."

"I'll say it for you... Deshaun. Trifling, dog-ass, Deshaun. I cursed again... I'm so sorry."

"I know that you're trying to eliminate the cursing and all but that one was justified."

"To make a long story short, I felt so bad and guilty for not telling her, that I started to overcompensate by going out of my way to pay for things that I knew she may have needed without consulting with her first. I was trying to help my friend, but I obviously just made things worse."

"So, let me get this straight... She's upset that you didn't allow her to figure out her own problem?"

"Correct."

"She has an issue with the fact that you didn't allow her to do something on her own?"

"Yes."

"That's interesting... Sounds like someone that I know," Mario paused and stared at Monique.

"Oh, my God... That sounds exactly like me."

"Bingo."

"Wow... I didn't even think about it like that."

"Baby, not only did you fail to put yourself in her shoes, you didn't even give her the opportunity to take the information that you were aware of and make her own decision on what to do with it. You deprived her of the one thing that you yourself cherish most."

"Which is what?"

"Independence. In the midst of everything that she's been through, I would bet my last that her pride is the thing that's been damaged the most. Her sense of independence as she once knew it has been torn away by her recent string of unfortunate circumstances."

Monique's jaws dropped. "Baby, you're right. I feel so horrible... What do I do now?"

"Besides apologize? Nothing."

"Huh?"

"You do absolutely nothing. The best thing anyone can do for Eve, at this point, is allow her to figure things out on her own. She has to do it, not only for her children, but also for her sense of self being. How can a person learn how to walk on their own if they always have a crutch to support them?"

"They can't," answered Monique.

"Sweetheart, it's time to let Eve learn to walk again."

CHAPTER EIGHTEEN

Eve strolled through the grocery store with a full list of demands. Beyond the household essentials, D.J. wanted Gatorade and beef jerky. Denisha wanted Swiss rolls and purple grapes. Eve just wanted to get in and out before the lines got long. After checking off what appeared to be the last item, Eve remembered that they were low on paper towels. She made a hard turn onto the paper goods aisle and collided into a gentleman's basket, knocking fruit, veggies, and protein bars all over the floor.

"Oh, my God. I'm so sorry. Let me get that for you," said Eve.

"No, it's fine. It was an accident... Don't worry about it." The man stopped and blinked twice. "Eve? Is that you?"

"Uh, yeah... Have we met before?"

"I'm Gary Lowe... We had a few classes together in high school."

Eve tried her best to remember. "Gary Lowe... Gary Lowe... Hold up... The science teacher, Mrs. Lowe's nephew, Gary?"

"Yep, that's me."

"Woooww. You look... Uhh... You look..."

"Different," said Gary.

Eve looked Gary over from head to toe. "Yes, different... You look good. Not saying you didn't look good back then."

Gary laughed. "It's okay... I didn't."

"Well, you said it not me... Did I just say that out loud?" Eve placed her hand at her chest. "That was so rude. I'm sorry."

"No, you're good. I was huge back then. After high school, I joined the Navy, started eating better and working out regularly. From there on, the weight just fell off."

"Wow. Good for you... So, are you still in the service?"

"No. My mom was diagnosed with stage four cancer two years ago. I was granted a temporary discharge to come home and take care of her. After she passed, I just didn't have it in me to go back."

"I'm so sorry to hear that."

"It's okay. She fought for as long as she could. At least I know she's not hurting anymore."

"Yeah, you're right... On a lighter note, what do you do now?"

"I'm a fireman," said Gary, lifting his chin in the air.

"Fireman, huh? Look at you. What department?"

"Long Beach... How about you? What've you been up to after all these years?"

"It'd probably take me all day to break it down to you."

Gary folded his monstrous arms and licked his lips. "I got time."

Eve blushed. "So, after high school I received an academic scholarship to Cal State Fullerton..."

"Nice."

"Thanks... Well, to sum it all up... Shortly after, I got married, had two beautiful children, and recently got a divorce. There it is—my life in a nutshell."

"I'm sorry to hear that... Not about your kids tho'. Kids are great... I mean as far as the divorce."

"It's fine... Actually, it was a huge blessing but that's a whole different story... Soooo? What about you? Married? Any kids of your own?"

"Actually, no to both."

Eve was surprised. "What?"

"Yeah... I know... I get that pretty often. People are always surprised when I tell them that?"

"What's wrong? You don't want any? Can't have any? Oops... that was so rude. Where are my manners today? Sorry."

Gary chuckled. "I definitely want kids. I just want the situation to be right. My parents' marriage wasn't the best. My father left when I was five years old. We never really had that good of a relationship. So, I guess a part of me just wants to make sure that history doesn't repeat itself... You know what I mean?"

Eve peeped at her watch. "I get it... Hey, I hate to be rude—again. Seems like I've been doing that this whole time, but I kind of have to get going."

"Yeah... Yeah... Sure, no problem. Sorry for holding you up."

"No, that was on me... Gary, it was great seeing you." Eve reached out to shake his hand, but he bypassed it, and gave her a big hug.

"Likewise... Hey, but you know what would be even greater?" asked Gary.

"What's that?"

"If I could see you again... Maybe a drink or two sometime soon? I'm not much of a drinker, but I'd make an exception if that meant a chance to hang out with you."

Eve smiled. "So, you're saying I look like an alcoholic?"

"No... No... Not at all. That came out all wrong. I'm sorry."

"Oh... Now you're the sorry one? I'm just kidding... But seriously... I don't know Gary. I have a lot going on in my life right now, and I just don't think I'm at a place where I'm ready to start dating."

"Dating? Who said anything about a date? I'm only offering you a drink or two." Gary smiled. "I'll tell you what, take my number down and think about it. No rush. No pressure."

Eve thought about it for a few seconds. "I can do that."

Gary entered his number into Eve's phone. "Well Eve, it was a pleasure. I look forward to hearing from you sooner than later."

Eve winked. "Maybe."

"Maybe is better than no, so I'll take It."

"Goodbye, Gary."

"See you later, Eve... Maybe."

CHAPTER NINETEEN

Na'Tosha paced back and forth outside of her apartment complex. Bo had been gone in her car for more than two days, and she was furious. Na'Tosha viciously pounded her foot against the pavement, while waiting for an Uber driver to arrive. She was already late for Monique's 8 a.m. hair appointment, which meant that all of her other client's appointments would be off as well. Bo's bullshit continued to put a damper on Na'Tosha's life.

"I can't believe this shit. How is it that I'm the one catching a ride, when I'm the one with the damn car? It's all right, tho'. Mmm hmm. I can't wait for that bitch to come home. I'm gon' slice and dice that ass up." Na'Tosha fought the air with an imaginary sword like a ninja in combat, demonstrating how she planned on cutting Bo.

As the newer modeled Ford Taurus approached, Na'Tosha frantically jumped into the backseat and immediately barked out orders, "I'm running late. Chop, chop, let's go."

The driver turned around and said, "Well, good morning, sunshine." Chaz, the Footlocker salesman was working his second job as a ride share driver. "You don't look so happy to see me," said Chaz with a sideways grin.

Na'Tosha didn't find his sarcasm entertaining. "Look, I don't have time today, okay. Please, turn around and drive the car."

"Why are you so rude? Were you neglected as child, or something?"

"First off, you're not a shrink—you're a shoe salesman, and apparently an Uber-slash-Lyft driver. So, stop counseling and start driving before I fuck around and give yo' ass one star."

The two mugged one another in a stare-off.

Chaz mumbled before turning around.

"Excuse me? Were you trying to say something? If so, speak up," yelled Na'Tosha.

Chaz chuckled before driving off.

Na'Tosha phoned Monique. *"Hey girl, I'm so sorry. I'm in an Uber now. I'm on my way."*

"An Uber?" asked Monique.

"Yeah, bitch that part. Bo good-fo-nothin' ass been gone in my car since the other day." Na'Tosha noticed Chaz watching her through the rearview mirror. *"Anyways, there's extra ears around. I'll be there in a few."*

"Okay girl, hurry up. I'm getting dizzy spinning around in your chair... Plus, I got to be looking good for Honolulu."

"I'm on my way now."

"Bye."

"Damn, you're all in my mouth. Turn up the radio or something."

"You mean turn up the radio, please?" replied Chaz.

Na'Tosha rolled her eyes. "Please? Nah, nigga. Turn up the radio now. The fuck."

Chaz slammed onto the breaks almost sending Na'Tosha flying into the front seat.

"You know what, I'm not having this shit. You're not disrespecting me in my own damn car. Now I don't know what yo' ass been going through this morning, and it really ain't none of my business..."

"You're right. It ain't none of yo' business."

The East Oakland in him unleashed before he even knew it. "What you're not gon' do is hop in my shit, acting hella rude and disrespectful. I've been nothing but nice to yo' out-of-pocket ass since you came into my job with yo' funky lil' attitude. If you can't respect that, you can walk."

Na'Tosha wasn't worried about what Chaz was saying. She was more focused on the way that he was saying it. Her panties moistened from the passion in his voice and conviction in his verbal onslaught. Chaz's sudden display of dominance sent her into another trance. His lips were moving, but the only voice Na'Tosha heard was the one inside her own head.

Aww shit. He big mad. I see Daddy got some back bone, tho'. Look at his fine ass all hot and bothered. Shit, snatch me by my throat then—not too hard tho', a bitch bruise easy. Snatch my clothes off—Nigga, pull my hair. I'm wit' all dat shit.

Na'Tosha stared with her mouth hanging open, but only momentarily. Once she recognized the increase of base in Chaz's voice, she quickly shook back. "I don't know who the fuck you think you're yelling at, but you got the right one today. Keep playing if you want to. Now turn around and drive along, Mr. One Star!"

Chaz didn't understand how a woman so attractive on the outside, could be so nasty on the inside. As bad as he wanted to cancel Na'-Tosha's ride, he didn't want to put her out so he continued with the trip.

The two rode in silence for the next few miles. Na'Tosha inserted AirPods into her ears as she tried to drift into a place of serenity. Her anxiety spiked tremendously since Bo's recent disappearance. The anticipation of being on her feet for the next twelve hours drove it up even higher. She searched for her emergency stash of Xanax. As Na'Tosha reached into her purse, Chaz deliberately thrashed onto the brakes. The majority of contents from her bag spewed throughout the backseat.

"We're here, buttercup," said Chaz with mockery.

Na'Tosha was enraged. She gathered her belongings and slammed the door before approaching the passenger window. "Oh, I almost forgot—I have a tip for you."

Chaz turned his head, looking straight ahead. "No thanks, I'm good."

"Please, I insist."

"Well, if you insist, there's a feature on the app where you can leave it."

"Nah, I'd rather leave it with you personally." Na'Tosha reached into her purse. "Here's your tip."

Chaz turned to see Na'Tosha's empty hand.

Instead, she raised her middle finger. "Stay out of dark alleys at night. A pretty lil' thang like you might get ya booty took. Ciao, nigga."

Na'Tosha backpedaled from the car with her middle finger still aimed in his direction.

Chaz dropped his head and laughed. "I swear her crazy ass need Jesus."

CHAPTER TWENTY

"Girl, I'm so sorry. I already know what you're going to say and trust me, I deserve it right about now. So, go ahead, and let me start on yo' head. At least we can be getting that out the way while you get on my ass," said Na'Tosha to Monique while preparing her station.

"It's okay. I won't be doing any chastising today—or any other day for that matter. Shit happens. If it's meant to be, I'm sure at some point, you two will work it out."

"Excuse me? Am I hearing this correctly? Mo's not doing anymore preaching? Mo's not telling me what I should or shouldn't be doing? Mo's not saying, I told you so?"

"That's right. From now on, Monique is focusing on what she has going on. I'm not forcing my opinion or advice on anyone that doesn't ask for it."

Monique took on the role of big sister. Whenever there was a crisis, she was the one to intervene. That assistance came with a hefty amount of criticism and ridicule.

"Well, say dat then, girl. Martin must really be dropping big D off in them draws and jaws."

Monique laughed. "You're so nasty... But girl, best believe Mario is definitely keeping a smile on my face in every single way."

"I'm happy to hear that. If anybody deserves it, honey, it's you."

"Aww," replied Monique.

"You're always there for everybody else, so it's good to finally know that someone is equipped to take care of you."

"Equipped is most definitely his middle name, boo." Monique high-fived Na'Tosha.

"Okaayy."

"But seriously tho'... Mario is amazing. He's kind, caring, intelligent, handsome... The way he makes me feel is unexplainable. I really think he might be the one."

"Well, g'on 'head, Mr. Right. I'm not gon' front... I'm lightweight jealous. Why I can't find me one like that?"

"Sweetie, you can have one. Mario has convinced me that good men still do exist."

"Well, lookie here. Somebody jumped on the 'good men still exist' train with lil' Ms. Eve. Just a few months ago, you was wit' me on team 'niggas ain't shit'. But I see Marvin den made you switch sides."

Monique laughed. "Girl, hush... Speaking of Eve... You still haven't heard from her?"

"Nope. Not since that day at The Pan... Have you?"

"Actually, I haven't—but she came into my job a while back and cursed me out tho'."

"Cursed you out for what?"

"For paying the kids tuition without her permission."

"I don't see the problem. That's what day-ones are supposed to do when times get rough."

"Yeah, but that was just the first part of it. She also let me know that she was fully aware that I knew about Deshaun and Ms. Skanky nurse... Hmmm, I wonder how she found that out?" Monique leaned backwards in her chair to make eye contact with Na'Tosha.

Avoiding eye contact, she said, "Yeah, I wonder how she found that out?"

"Mmm hmm, yeah, I wonder how, too—I'm not mad though. I'm kind of glad that it all finally came out. Carrying that burden was eating away at my conscience. Right now, I'm giving her some space, but when Mario and I get back from Hawaii, I'm going to reach out and make things right. I miss her."

"I can't even front. I miss her ass, too. You know what? I need to be making my way over there. Life is way too short for the bullshit. We're sisters. Ain't no need for us to be beefin'."

"Speaking of beef—it's some walking in as we speak," said Monique.

Bo timidly inched into the salon, holding a bouquet of five-dollar grocery store flowers.

Monique and Na'Tosha stopped and turned as Bo awkwardly approached.

"What's up, Mo," said Bo.

"Hey."

"Good morning, baby." Bo handed Na'Tosha the flowers.

She slapped the flowers out of Bo's hand. "Where the fuck have you been in my car, Bo?"

"Baby, not like this. Can we talk outside?"

"Talk for what? Give me my damn keys."

Monique saw the rage brewing in Na'Tosha's eyes. "It's okay, Na'Tosha. Go ahead. I don't mind waiting."

Bo apprehensively led the way as Na'Tosha cocked her arm back pretending to slap Bo upside the head. Immediately after stepping outside, Na'Tosha stopped in her tracks when she saw "cheater," "fuck girl," "I hate yo stupid ass," "fuck you," and "run back to the bitch" keyed all over her silver Altima. Her eyes watered, knees trembled, and lips quivered.

"Baby, now I know what you're thinking but this isn't what it looks like. It's actually a funny story... So, Jermaine's baby momma, Carla had seen us driving down Crenshaw on our way to the homie C house. Jermaine was driving because five-o got behind us earlier, and he the only one in the car with a license. So bam, I pulled over and let him drive real quick. This crazy bitch Carla saw the home girl Pam in the backseat... Baby, you remember the homie, Pam? Anyways, she thought Pam..."

Na'Tosha let out a deranged shriek from the pit of her stomach. "What the fuck did you do to my car."

"Baby, I'm trying to explain—just hear me out." Bo paced back and forth trying to remember her scripted lie.

Na'Tosha pulled out the baby nine-millimeter pistol kept handily inside of her fanny pack. She cocked the gun and pointed in Bo's direction. "You want to play wit' me, muthafucka. I told yo' bitch-ass stop playin' wit' me."

Terror filled Bo's eyes. "I'm not playing. On the dead homies. Please, don't shoot me. Baby, please."

"You finna be dead right wit' they ass."

Bo back-stepped with her arms stretched out in fear of Na'Tosha's next move. "Baby, it don't gotta be like this. I'm getting it fixed. Just trust me."

Monique patiently waited in her chair, scrolling through her Instagram timeline. She hated seeing her friends dealing with drama from their significant others. Deep down, Na'Tosha was a sweet girl and deserved much more than Bo could offer. It took every fiber in Monique's body to refrain from helping Na'Tosha double-team Bo's good-for-nothing ass. But, after vowing to mind her own business, all she could do was support from a distance.

In the blink of an eye, the thunderous sound of gunshots echoed from the parking lot. Glass shattered as bullets ripped through various stores within the strip mall. Every patron in proximity ducked for cover.

Once the shots came to a halt, Monique's "big sisterly" instincts kicked in. *Na'Tosha... Na'Tosha... Please, tell me you didn't just do what I think you did?* She quickly got up from the salon floor and rushed outside.

CHAPTER TWENTY-ONE

Eve took a deep look into the mirror and barely recognized herself. Thick bags formed underneath her eyes and wrinkles had developed throughout her face. The fifteen stress-related pounds she lost caused her to look malnourished. Life was really kicking her butt.

The obstacles of being a working single parent were catching up to her. Bills came so often that Eve avoided checking the mailbox. Every time she paid one, an even larger bill followed. To add insult to injury, Christmas was right around the corner. Sadly, Santa wouldn't be leaving much underneath the tree.

Eve swallowed two Percocets and chased it down with a swig of vodka. Makeup ran down her cheeks as tears flowed from her eyes. She was tempted to call Monique and Na'Tosha for support but didn't feel comfortable reaching out. Especially, after she'd been secluded for the past few months. She doubled down, remembering how they'd both crossed boundaries, no longer deserving to be involved in her life.

Deep down, the grudges bothered her. Not a day went by that the kids didn't ask about one of their aunties. Blood couldn't have made them any closer. Yet, Eve's pride wouldn't let her give in. She'd seen, and repeatedly ignored, calls and texts from both ladies. The more Eve ignored them, the worse she felt about it. Alcohol and pills, her new best friends, helped numb those emotions.

Eve reached for a pair of scissors sitting on the sink. She took the sharp object and pressed it against her jugular. Thoughts of suicide plagued her mind. Eve contemplated if life was even worth living anymore. At that moment, a scripture came to mind. Deuteronomy 31:6 *Be strong and of good courage, fear not, nor be affrighted of them: for Jehovah thy God, he it is that doth go with thee; he will not fail thee, nor forsake thee.* It was her late grandmother's favorite verse to recite.

Eve knew that this was all a test, and with the grace of God, soon would pass. D.J. and Denisha's livelihood relied on her being in a sound mind frame, and there was no way that she was going to let them down.

Eve took a deeper look into the mirror, this time, she recognized herself. What she saw was a child of God. A strong, independent mother of two, created in the image of God Himself. Eve felt the spirit of strength come over her. She removed the scissors from her neck and faced them upright.

In an act of liberation, Eve took the scissors and hacked off several inches of her big, bouncy, curly afro. Then, she boldly marched to the toilet with a fierce pep in her step, dumped the hair, vodka, and remaining pills into the water and watched as the poison swirled its way down.

She turned on the shower and waited until the temperature was scorching hot. Once it reached its peak, Eve scrubbed away all of the pain, stress, and depression that had been making her life miserable. The devil, nor his advocate, Deshaun, would continue to have dominion over her. Eve shut the water off, leaving all of the old drama from the past behind.

After drying off, she gracefully glided into the closet and grabbed a dress that'd never been worn. Eve styled her new hairdo into something cute and edgy. Upon completion, she admired the results. She held her head high and smiled at herself. Eve took a few selfies as a keepsake for her moment of triumph.

While scrolling through the phone, she sat on the edge of her bed and decided to make a call.

A deep voice answered, *"Hello."*

"Hey, it's Eve. Does that offer for a drink still stand?

CHAPTER TWENTY-TWO

"Okay Jimerson, let's make it quick. Spread your cheeks, give me three squats, and cough after each one. When you're done, place your hands behind your back, and follow the yellow line down the hallway until you reach the next station. You'll have your fingerprints and mugshots taken there," a burly female correctional officer said. "Do I make myself clear?"

The screeching sound of police sirens replayed through Na'Tosha's mind. Everything from there on was a blur. She was too traumatized to cry—or, even think straight for that matter. The last thing Na'Tosha remembered was Bo's pitiful face pleading for mercy. Was she dead? Did anyone else get hit? Was it even worth it? There were so many questions that needed answers. For now, exposing her asshole to a complete stranger was first on the agenda. The absolute, most degrading and disgusting thing you could ever ask a person to do. That's the part about being a criminal they fail to mention.

Na'Tosha was a hothead but was definitely not about that jail life. This was a woman who was accustomed to weekly pedicures and manicures, refused to eat leftovers, and showered three times daily, all because she hated the feeling of sweat. Na'Tosha gagged as she held the reused pair of state issued panties to the light.

"Hurry up and get dressed, Jimerson. Fingerprinting is waiting for you."

After having her fingerprints taken, the correctional officer handed Na'Tosha a sack lunch and escorted her into a holding cell. Inside of the bag were an orange, a small bag of plain Lay's potato chips, and a dry bologna sandwich. Na'Tosha peeled back the bread and exposed the huge chunk of processed meat. Tears fell from her eyes. She couldn't fathom the idea of spending the rest of her life in captivity. Na'Tosha's father was given a life sentence when she was a teenager and that, along with visiting Bo, was her only experiences with anyone being incarcerated. Na'Tosha sobbed as she nestled against the dirty, concrete slab. She closed her eyes and prayed that this whole ordeal was just one huge nightmare.

A few hours passed and Na'Tosha was still there. The notion of it all being a bad dream had been eliminated. The bright lights, hard surface, and chilling air made it nearly impossible to fall asleep. Three women had joined her inside of the receiving tier. One woman skittishly paced the floor, while the other two shared animated stories of their lives as prostitutes. Na'Tosha tried hard to maintain her composure. But, the fear of the unknown left her a nervous wreck.

A male correctional officer appeared at the door. Behind him was a short, older gentleman dressed in black slacks and a blue-collared shirt. A gold LAPD detective's badge dangled around his neck. The correctional officer opened the door and signaled for Na'Tosha.

"Na'Tosha Jimerson. Come with me." The detective led Na'Tosha into an office located near the entrance of the jail. "Have a seat but don't get too comfortable."

Na'Tosha wiped tears from her eyes. "Can I please make a phone call?"

The detective shuffled through a stack of folders on top of his desk. "Where's that file? I just had it—oh, there it is." He removed a document from a folder, signed it, and handed it to Na'Tosha. "No, you cannot make a phone call. Now, sign here."

"Please, sir. I need to call my family. I don't belong here. Why can't I just make one call?"

"Because you're going home... That's why."

Na'Tosha was shocked. "I am?"

"Yes, due to lack of sufficient evidence. We don't have a victim or witnesses willing to cooperate. Your gun was warm when we arrived, which indicated that it had been fired, but lucky for you, we didn't find any shell casings to support that theory. All we found was you sitting on the ground, rocking back and forth with the gun in your hand, in some sort of demonic trance repeatedly saying, 'Imma kill that bitch'."

For the first time in her whole life, Na'Tosha was speechless. The only words that her mouth could utter were, "Oh, wow."

"Oh wow, is right—now ma'am, once you sign that paper, you're free to go. But I do strongly suggest that you stay far away from whoever it is that you were referring to." The detective handed Na'Tosha a pen. "Your firearm is registered, you've never been in any trouble, you operate a successful business, and the neighboring owners near your shop had nothing but good things to say about you. It seems like you have a lot going for yourself. Don't throw it all away over some loser. Now, you be careful, Ms. Jimerson. The next time, I assure you, you won't be so lucky." The detective winked at Na'Tosha.

She knew that he was going against protocol to show this level of leniency. "Sir, that's something I promise you won't ever have to worry about."

"For your sake, I sure hope so... You'll be able to retrieve your weapon and other belongings at the property window upfront. Good luck, Ms. Jimerson."

Na'Tosha's prayers had been answered. "Thank you, sir. Thank you."

The detective accompanied Na'Tosha to the property window. The two shook hands and went their separate ways. Just like that, Na'Tosha was free.

Monique greeted her in the lobby, waiting there since shortly after the cop car hauled her best friend away.

Na'Tosha collapsed into Monique's arms. Five years of being lied to, cheated on, manipulated, undermined, underappreciated, and undervalued were put to rest as she wept her tired, little heart out. Na'Tosha loved Bo, but not more than her freedom. This incident was the straw that broke the camel's back.

CHAPTER TWENTY-THREE

Monique and Mario were in a black Cadillac Escalade limo on their way to the airport. A five-day romantic holiday vacation to paradise awaited them.

Mario uncorked a bottle of champagne in celebration of the occasion.

Monique's excitement poured out as the bubbly sizzled inside of their glasses.

"Oh, my God." She clapped her hands. "I'm so excited."

Mario kissed Monique. "So am I, baby." He raised his glass.

"Cheers to the first of many vacations together."

She touched her glass with his. "Cheers," replied Monique before sipping from the ice-cold glass of Ace of Spades.

Mario was everything Monique ever wanted in a man. And he was proving to be the rock that she so heroically needed.

"Lately, I've had so much going on. From Grandmommy, to work, to drama with my friends... I couldn't have gotten through any of it without your amazing support. Thanks, baby. I so desperately needed this."

"You're welcome, sweetheart. These past few months with you in it have been amazing. I'm excited to see what the future holds for us."

Mario leaned in for another kiss. Only this time it wasn't just a peck that he was after.

The two zealously engaged in foreplay, leading to him unsnapping Monique's bra just as her phone buzzed in her purse.

"Hold up a second, baby. It's Na'Tosha... Let me answer this," said Monique before accepting the call.

"Hello?"

"Hey, Honolulu boo."

"Hey, boo."

"Y'all make it to the airport yet?"

"We're on our way now. What's up? Everything okay?"

"Yeah, girl. I'm good. I'm going down to the dealership to check some cars out a little later... Other than that, I'm okay."

Mario slowly removed his shirt and motioned for Monique to come closer with his index finger.

"Okay... Well, let me go... I'm kind of in the middle of something. If you know what I mean?"

"Y'all so nasty... Have fun, girl. Let me know when y'all land."

"I will, girl... Bye."

Monique ended the call and seductively removed her dress while hypnotizing Mario with rhythmic body motions. "Sorry about that... Now, where were we?"

She leaned forward and brushed her tongue against his six-pack, watching Mario's testosterone rage into a craze. Monique slowly made her way down towards his beltline. As she loosened his belt, the phone rang again.

"Baby, your phone's ringing again."

Monique's focus was solely on removing that belt. "I hear it... Let it ring."

Mario smiled. "Baby, they're just going to keep calling... Answer it."

"Okay. Okay. I'll answer it... This better be important." Monique grabbed the phone. "What the hell does Rebecca want?" She took a deep breathe before answering it.

"Hello."

"Hello, Ms. Harris. You have an important message from—"

"—I'm on vacation. I don't care. Whatever it is can wait. Bye." Monique ended the call before Rebeca could continue.

"That was kind of rude," said Mario.

"Yeaaah—buuut—I'm on vacation, and I kind of don't care. As a matter of fact, I'm turning my ringer off." Monique silenced the phone and tossed it onto the floor.

"A little spunky today aren't we, Ms. Harris?"

"Damn skippy."

Mario laughed as he caressed Monique's breasts. "Just the way I like it."

The two continued along with their discrete sexual encounter. Both got an extra thrill from pleasuring one another without the driver's knowledge. The hour-long drive to the airport provided plenty of time to get freaky. Once done, the lovebirds cuddled, sipped more champagne, and enjoyed the relaxing R&B music streaming through the speakers.

Monique's topless body snuggled into Mario's bare chest and arms. His strength and warmth provided tranquility. The driver began lowering the partition to notify the couple of their arrival to the airport.

Mario yelled for him not to do so. "No. No. Not yet."

The driver raised the partition back up.

"We are so bad," said Monique.

Mario kissed her shoulder. "Yeah, but the sex is so good."

He attempted to lick his way to the back of her neck, but Monique pleaded for him to stop.

"No, baby come on. We're here. Put your shirt on."

They both got fully dressed and exited the vehicle. The driver graciously unloaded their matching Louis Vuitton luggage onto the curb.

Mario reached into his pocket and handed him a twenty-dollar bill. "Here you go, big man."

"Thanks, sir," said the limo driver.

Mario grabbed the bags and headed towards the airport's entrance. He paused before reaching into his pocket a second time. This time a fifty-dollar bill emerged. "Hey, take this too... You might want to let that backseat air out a little bit. It got pretty steamy back there."

The driver smiled and happily accepted the additional tip. "No worries. I'll take care of it. You two have a safe trip."

Monique and Mario made their way to the ticket counter. Monique searched her purse looking for identification. A look of panic graced her face.

"Something wrong, sweetheart?" asked Mario.

"I left my phone in the limo. Oh, Lord... I hope he's still out there."

Monique bolted towards the entrance. Fortunately, the driver was on his way in with the phone. "Can't go too far without this now, can you?"

"Oh, my God. I almost had a heart attack... Thank you so much."

The driver tipped his hat. "You're welcome, ma'am."

Monique turned the ringer on and noticed a barrage of missed notifications flooding the screen. The messages that garnered the most attention were from her grandmother's senior living facility. Monique dialed the number and waited for a response.

She dropped to her knees when the staff member notified her that Ida Mae Eason had passed away. Monique screamed at the top of her lungs as the nurse tried to explain the details of Grandmommy's death. The cries from her broken heart were heard throughout the airport. Mario immediately rushed to his woman's aid. Monique's inconsolable body laid flat against the lobby floor. Mario held her limp torso in the same exact way he'd done in the limousine, moments prior. Only this time, the joy was replaced with pain. And a day that began in celebration, ended in tragedy.

THE FUNERAL

Ida Mae's death had a great impact on many people. Individuals from all walks of life gathered in her memory. Grief and sorrow filled the church.

Mario held Monique's hands while they sat on the front row of the church. He noted how well Monique had been holding up since the day of receiving the unfortunate news. Her display of strength and fortitude increased his deep admiration. However, Mario was right by Monique's side in case that courage ever wavered.

Relatives and friends lined the pews. Monique looked behind her and spotted Na'Tosha from a distance. The two blew each other kisses. She was grateful for Na'Tosha's unconditional love. She surveyed the other side of the church. On the back row was an important group of people she hadn't seen in quite a while. She smiled at the very sight of Eve, D.J. and Denisha.

Shortly after, the pastor approached the altar and gave an impactful eulogy. The message was based on the importance of family, salvaging bonds, and letting go of the past. These points all resonated with Monique and her friends. Monique knew the three of them had been dealing with different forms of holding on for too long. She knew she was holding on too long to guilt, Eve was holding on too long to sorrow, and Na'Tosha was holding on too long to dysfunction. Although, they'd already made strides towards tackling these issues, Monique felt the pastor's words provided a sense of confirmation.

When the service was over, everyone gathered outside. Mario anchored Monique while she received condolences from passersby.

Na'Tosha sauntered over with dark shades covering her dreary eyes. "Hey, girl. Are you okay?"

Monique was saddened but maintained her composure. "I'm well... Thanks, boo."

While receiving a strong embrace from Na'Tosha, Monique noticed Eve whispering something to the kids before venturing the ladies' way. The tension made the thirty-foot trek seem like a mile to Monique.

Once Eve made it over, all three ladies were silent. Several seconds passed as their energies reconnected. To Monique's surprise, Eve broke the ice by extending her arms. The other two immediately followed suit. The trio was reunited. Words, explanations, and apologies weren't necessary. Everything that they'd been enduring individually—and collectively—poured out onto each other's shoulders.

All friendships go through tests. Theirs wasn't any different. But true bonds always find a way to stand the test of time.

CHAPTER TWENTY-FOUR

It'd been a month since the funeral. Monique stayed busy in order to keep her mind occupied. Eve and Na'Tosha frequently checked on her, but conflicting schedules interfered with them all being together at once. A girl's night out was long overdue. The three decided to link up at one of their favorite happy hour spots called, The Green Onion. Eve and Monique arrived around the same time. Ms. Na'Tosha was late as usual.

"Hey, girl... How have you been holding up?" asked Eve.

Monique's face displayed uneasiness but her Ida Mae-like pride wouldn't allow her to convey it. "I'm good... Just taking it one day at a time."

"Aww. Honey, come here." Eve hugged Monique. "Everything is going to be okay."

"I know... I just miss her crazy self so much."

Eve smiled. "Girl, now you know she's looking down at us right now wondering why we don't have any men with us."

Monique laughed before doing her best Ida Mae impersonation, "Why y'all ain't never got no man around? I'm starting to worry 'bout y'all. Y'all ain't doin' that ol' carpet munching stuff they doing nowadays now, is y'all? I can just hear her now..."

Eve laughed. "No... Remember when she found out that Na'Tosha liked girls?"

"Girl, do I?"

Flashback...

The year was 2003 and sixteen-year-old Na'Tosha was on her way home from school. She was holding hands with one of the coolest kids at Crenshaw High. Traymeka Turner a.k.a. "Tray-T" was a young Phenom in the local sport's community. She was an All-American basketball and track star and Na'Tosha had a huge crush on her since the ninth grade. Although she was strictly into boys at the time, something about Tray-T struck Na'Tosha's interest.

One day, during sophomore year, Na'Tosha finally mustered enough courage to slip Tray-T a cute little love note. Tray-T accepted Na'Tosha's advance, and from there, they began to date, keeping their relationship under wraps.

Ida Mae was on the front porch playing cards with her neighbor, Mrs. Johnson. The two gossiped, drank Old English Malt Liquor out of straws, and listened to Al Green.

Mrs. Johnson spotted Na'Tosha first and tapped Ida Mae's arm and pointed.

"What in the ring-a-round the rosie, devilish, mannish confused-ness goin' on over there?" Ida Mae said, peering over the rim of her glasses.

"Shame on them, Ida. Ain't that Claritha Anne grandbaby?" asked Mrs. Johnson.

Ida squinted to get a better look. "Girl, it sho is."

Ida Mae snatched her glasses off her face when Na'Tosha and Tray-T stepped towards each other for a kiss and screamed from across the street, "Na'Tosha."

The two girls stepped back from each other and continued down the street.

"Na'Tosha, yo' ass hear me callin' you," Ida Mae yelled again.

Na'Tosha stood frozen. "Shit." She took in a deep breath. "Yeeesss, Ms. Ida?"

"Get yo' lil' fast tail over here. And bring me a switch."

Na'Tosha went to the smallest tree she could find and grabbed a puny limb.

Tray-T wisely used her All-American speed to sprint in the opposite direction.

"Girl, hurry up. Make sho you take all them leaves off too."

"Yes, Ms. Ida," replied Na'Tosha.

Ida turned and whispered to Mrs. Johnson. "You know I wondered why that girl breath always smelled like fish."

• • •

Eve and Monique laughed hysterically. They hadn't shared that story in years.

Na'Tosha arrived as their giggles came to an end. "Good vibes, I see. Sorry, I'm late... What did I miss?"

"Your ass is always late," said Eve in a playful tone.

"Oh, well. Being this fine, takes time, honey."

"We were just talking about the time Grandmommy found out about your little secret," said Monique.

"Girl, she tore my ass up with that damn switch. Crazy thing about it, I was almost seventeen and damn near grown. Ms. Ida gave zero fucks, okay."

All three ladies laughed.

"Hold up... Hold up, tho', Ms. Monique. What about that time she caught Phillip Conners in yo' room? I bet you forgot all about that one, now didn't you?"

Eve waved her hand, flagging down the bartender. "Phillip Conners? I haven't heard that name in so long."

"Oh, Lord... Please, don't take me back to that night," said Monique.

FLASHBACK...

Seventeen-year-old Monique was inside her bedroom with her high school sweetheart, Phillip Conners. The night was supposed to be special for the two. Monique planned to finally give Phillip her virginity. They'd kissed, and played around, but never went all the way.

However, the golden opportunity presented itself when Ida Mae notified Monique that she'd be gone longer than usual on this particular night.

Phillip, who claimed to be an expert in the lovemaking department, sat on the edge of the bed, fidgeting with a Lifestyle condom, while glancing at the door every few seconds.

"Are you sure your granny not gon' pop up?"

"She won't. First, she's going to visit my paw-paw at the hospital. Then, she's going to be at bingo until at least eleven o'clock. We're good for a couple hours."

"All right, because remember the last time I called after ten o'clock, she said that she was gon' bite my dingaling off, suck it for a minute, then spit it back at me if I ever called her house that late again."

"I know... I know... Relax. She's not coming home any time soon." Monique looked at Phillip with puppy dog eyes. "But, I mean... You can leave if you're scared."

"Stop playing. I ain't scared of nothing."

"Okay then... Stop trippin'."

The two kissed with Phillip, the self-proclaimed pro, awkwardly fiddling with Monique's bra, before finally unhooking it five minutes later.

Soon after, Ida Mae kicked the bedroom door off of the hinges. She wielded a knife in one hand and a belt in the other. Ida Mae stared into Phillip's eyes. In an evil villain voice she said, "Come here, lil' boy. I'm finna cut dat lil' dingaling off."

The terror in Phillip's eyes was as if he'd seen Michael Myers. Phillip hopped up, face-dived out of Monique's second story window and summersaulted onto the front lawn, dashing down the street faster than Usain Bolt.

Monique wasn't so fortunate. She hollered as Ida Mae's thick leather belt nearly beat the black off her butt cheeks.

• • •

Stories of Ida Mae's antics never seemed to get old. Eve and Na'Tosha cracked up like it was their first time hearing it.

"Phillip wouldn't even look my way after that," said Monique.

"Shit... I wouldn't have either," said Na'Tosha.

"Well, my most memorable experience with Ms. Ida was a little different. Do y'all remember the time when Qwaniesha nem tried to jump me after cheerleading practice?" asked Eve.

"What?" Monique pounded her fist. "Still 'til this day I can't stand her big, black ass. Oops, my bad." She covered her mouth after cursing.

"I'll never forget... Mo, you were sick that day, and Na'Tosha had just got kicked off the squad after getting suspended for stealing Mrs. Coleman's makeup out of her purse."

"I sho did. Dat bitch had MAC... I needed that, okkaayy."

"Girl, you're so crazy. Anyways... I was coming out of the gym, and there she was, waiting on me..."

FLASHBACK...

Seventeen-year-old Eve exited the school gymnasium after a long practice. Being captain of the cheerleading squad required a lot. After jumping, kicking, and flipping, homework still needed to be done. Eve's goals were to get home, complete her assignments, do chores, and catch a couple re-run episodes of her favorite show, Moesha.

Outside waiting for Eve was the school's female bully. Qwaniesha Spikes was big, mean, and nasty. Every girl, and half the boys, at Crenshaw High was scared of her.

Eve saw Qwaniesha and her goons blocking the playground exit. She sensed that the click of low-lives were up to no good. She firmly gripped her books and proceeded towards the gate.

Qwaniesha spat at Eve's feet. "What's up, bitch?"

Eve rolled her eyes. "What do you want, Qwaniesha?"

"I heard you call yourself liking my man?"

"Your man, who?" asked Eve.

"Mookie... Bitch, you know who I'm talking about."

Eve laughed. She tried not to but couldn't resist. "Mookie Wilson?"

"Did I say something funny? Yeah, bitch, Mookie Wilson...That's my man. Now keep yo' ugly ass away from him or Imma beat that ass."

Mookie Wilson was the cute starting point guard for Crenshaw High. He and Eve talked but weren't an official couple yet. Either way,

Mookie wouldn't have been caught anywhere near the likes of Qwaniesha Spikes.

"Okay... Whatever you say, Qwaniesha." Eve tried to maneuver past when Qwaniesha knocked the books out of her hands. She gave Qwaniesha a cold stare.

But Qwaniesha and her squad were ready to rumble. "I wish you would, bitch. What you wanna do?"

Eve calmly retrieved her books from the ground.

"Yeah... That's what I thought, bitch." Saliva from the corner of Qwaniesha's crusty mouth splatted onto Eve's face.

Ida Mae just so happened to be driving by the school on her way to the store when out of the corner of her eye, she noticed a group of large females. After taking a closer look, she realized that little Eve was in the middle. "Oh, hell naw. Them over-grown heffas ain't finna jump on my baby." Ida Mae parked the car and reached into the glove compartment, grabbing a head scarf, and some Vaseline. She applied the slippery substance onto her face and tied up her hair. Ida Mae burst towards the crowd. "Who do y'all think y'all finna jump on? Not that one."

"Old lady, who the fuck are you?" asked Qwaniesha.

"I'm the old lady that's finna whoop yo' ass if you touch my baby. So, if you think you're bad, g'on 'head fat, black, ugly heffa."

Qwaniesha's wrath didn't have an age limit. She bucked up, getting into Ida Mae's face. "Yo' old ass ain't gon' do shit."

Little did Qwaniesha know, that old-ass lady didn't have an age limit either. Ida Mae pulled out a can of pepper spray and unloaded the entire thing on Qwaniesha and her crew. The party of five screamed in agony as the spray scorched every exposed inch of their bodies.

After realizing she'd just committed at least five felonies, Ida Mae made a run for it. "Hurry up, baby. We gotta roll."

Both Eve and Ida jumped into the car and sped off.

• • •

The ladies were in tears as Eve finished the story, "Ms. Ida was a G... She didn't care how old or young you were. If you ever disrespected her... She was going off. Periodt."

"Y'all took me back with these high school stories," said Monique.

Eve sipped from her rum and coke. "Sooo... Speaking of high school, I've been kind of, sort of seeing somebody that we went to high school with."

Na'Tosha braced herself, gripping the table. "Wait... Wait... Wait... You've been seeing somebody? Did I just hear that correctly?"

"Yes, you heard that correctly."

Monique's eyes lit up while quickly swiveling around in her chair. "Details. Details. Girl, who is it?"

"Gary Lowe."

Monique scratched her head. "Did he graduate with us?"

"Yes."

Na'Tosha squinted and stared off into the distance. "Gary... Gary... Gary... Nope doesn't ring a bell. The only Gary that I remember was my junior year science teacher ashy, fat, stinky, ugly nephew with the braces and messed up afro".

"Bingo." Eve stirred the ice inside of her empty glass. "That's him."

Na'Tosha spat her drink out. "Eve, what the hell? I know times are hard and all but got-damn."

"Y'all can't be talking about the same Gary, right?" asked Monique.

Eve shrugged her shoulders. "It's the same Gary."

Na'Tosha couldn't believe her ears, raising her hands towards the sky and praying. "Lord, now you know a bitch been sinning, but please just hear ya girl out one more time. Whatever this hoe Eve going through, Heavenly Father, fix it. In Jesus Name."

Eve nodded her head. "Gary has changed a lot since high school. He's a great man. I'm thinking about introducing him to the kids pretty soon."

"Well, as long as you're happy, we're happy. Isn't that right, Na'-Tosha?"

Na'Tosha closed her eyes and started praying in tongues, "Lord, humshallahdahumshalladah..."

Monique nudged Na'Tosha's shoulder. "I said, isn't that right?"

Na'Tosha pretended to cry. "Yes, boo... As long... As you're happy."

Monique rolled her eyes. "You're so damn dramatic... Anyways... Eve, do you have a picture of him?"

"Actually, I do." Eve pulled out her phone and showed the ladies a photo of the new and approved Gary.

"Damn, my bad, girl… That ain't the Gary that I remember," said Na'Tosha.

Monique also expressed her approval. "Oh… He is fine."

Eve blushed. "I told y'all that he's changed."

"I can't wait to meet him," said Monique.

Na'Tosha playfully licked her lips. "Shit, I can't wait either."

Eve snatched her phone. "Un uhh. Y'all thirsty bitches better back up."

Monique grabbed Eve's hand. "No, seriously… I'm happy for you."

"Thanks… We should double date sometime… Wait hold up… I'm sorry, Na'Tosha. That was rude of me. Let's make it a triple date and bring Bo, and we'll all go do something fun together."

Monique turned and ducked her head. She'd forgotten that Eve wasn't in the loop about Na'Tosha's latest hiccup with Bo.

"Ain't no more Bo, bih," said Na'Tosha in the voice of rap artist Plies.

"Oh, no. What happened?" asked Eve.

Na'Tosha gulped down her Hennessy

Monique went ahead and handed hers over to NaTosha as well.

Na'Tosha polished off Monique's Long Island Iced Tea and let out a huge burp. "One second—hey, bartender… Another round." She looked at Eve. "Bitch, I need to be extra buzzin' to relive that horror story."

CHAPTER TWENTY-FIVE

Eve paced along the bleachers of St. Joseph's gymnasium. D.J's championship basketball game was minutes from tip off, and her nerves were worse than his. She spotted Coach Nelson from across the gym and saw him waving at her. She also saw Deshaun coming in her direction, obviously headed toward his girlfriend who was seated a few rows away.

"I need to holla at you real quick. Let's step over here for a second," said Deshaun with flared nostrils.

Eve cautiously followed him to an empty section of the bleachers.

"Damn, coach Nelson, too? Now I see why D.J. gets so much playing time... And all this time I thought it was his jump shot."

Eve rolled her eyes. "Deshaun, what are you talking about?"

"I mean, it's obvious for the world to see that y'all fuckin'. I just would've thought for the sake of D.J., you'd keep it more on the low... But that'd be too much like right, now, wouldn't it?"

"Whatever, Deshaun... I'm not screwing Coach Nelson. I'd never put my son—"

"—Our son. Get that shit right."

Eve took a deep breath before rolling her eyes. "Excuse me... Put our son in that position. But if it just so happened that I was screwing coach Nelson, it wouldn't be any of your or the world's business."

"Man, fuck all that... What's up with this clown you're bringing around our kids? Yo' desperate ass finally met someone that takes you half way serious, and the first thing you do is let them come in your house, and bring them around your kids?"

"Correction... You're wrong. There were a few other places I let him cum in before he actually came over."

"What kind of bitch brings dudes they barely know around their kids?"

Eve folded her arms. "A grown one."

Deshaun clinched his fist and took a step towards Eve.

"What are you going to do, Deshaun, hit me? You're going beat me up at your son's game in front of all these people? Huh, tough guy? Go ahead, then... Do what you have to do?"

"Nah, I'm just going to hit you where it hurts. I'm getting full custody of the kids. You're not bringing random-ass niggas around my kids. That's out."

Deshaun's threats no longer held any merit for Eve. She simply chuckled. "Go ahead... Shit, I could use the break. The early mornings cooking breakfast, packing lunches, commuting for hours in L.A. traffic to get them to and from school, doing homework at night, soup and medicine when they're sick. If that's what you want to do, be my guest."

"Damn, is the D that good that you'd just give up on your kids like that?"

"Although the D is indeed that good, I'd never give up on my kids. But what I am giving up on is you thinking you can control and dictate how I operate my life. When you had a baby on the side while we were married, I didn't like it. When you brought ya lil' white whore, who you was cheating on me the whole time with, around our kids, I didn't like it. But guess what? I dealt with it. As long as she's not putting them in harm's way, I have no other choice but to keep my thoughts and opinions to myself—"

Deshaun interrupted, "—Here you go with the—"

"—I'm—not—finished. As I was saying... I do a phenomenal job with our kids. There's nothing on this earth more important to me than being their mother. I put them first, second, and third. I'd never bring a man around that I hadn't screened up, down, in, and out before giving him the privilege to even set eyes on my babies. So, what I'm going to need you to do is go back over there wit' ya lil' Barbie bimbo, and stay far the hell out of my business as humanly possible. But before you do go, is there anything else you'd like to discuss besides who I'm screwing? If so, go right ahead... If not, I'd like to watch our son's basketball game."

Deshaun stood with his mouth hanging open, unable to generate a response.

Eve gave him a few more seconds to reply. "I'll take that as a no... Have a blessed day, sir."

Deshaun slinked back to his seat with his tail tucked.

Eve sat down and took a deep breath. She'd finally built enough courage to stand up to the boogie man. The days of succumbing to Deshaun's nitpicking were over.

CHAPTER TWENTY-SIX

Na'Tosha searched aisle after aisle looking for the car that matched her swag the most. Getting around had become extremely difficult since Bo destroyed her 2013 silver Nissan Altima, affectionately known as Bonnie. Throughout the years, Na'Tosha's heavy foot and Bo's negligence caused several issues to the car. The radiator leaked, two motor mounts were cracked, and the air conditioning didn't work. In all actuality, Bonnie being totaled was a blessing in disguise.

She strolled through the row of luxury pre-owned vehicles, smelling the fresh leather, adding to her excitement. One car in particular caught her attention.

"Hello, I'm Barry." A salesman approached. "Nice car, right?" said Barry.

"Yaaasss. It's so bomb."

"That there is a candy-apple-red, two-thousand-ninteen, Mercedes S-six-three four-matic A-M-G V-eight twin turbo, with six-hundred twenty-one horsepower."

"I don't know what none of that means, but it's cute, tho'."

Barry brushed his arm across Na'Tosha's back. It means that it has a lot of power... You sure a little lady like yourself can handle something that big and strong?"

"If it ain't big and strong, boo, I don't want it."

Barry smiled. "Confidence... I like that."

"Yep... And plenty of it."

Barry gently grabbed Na'Tosha's hand and caressed it. "Let's see if you feel the same way after we take this puppy for a spin... Oh, and I love your nails by the way. Fabulous color choice."

Something about Barry's touchy-feely behavior gave NaTosha a flirty vibe. "Thank you, big Barry. Let's go see what this thang do."

After returning from the test drive, the two landed in Barry's office. Na'Tosha filled out paperwork and provided her driver's license.

Barry took the documents and excused himself into a different part of the dealership.

He returned shortly with a concerned look on his face. "Na'-Tosha... Hey... Umm... So, I ran a credit check, and it seems that we have a slight dilemma."

"What kind of dilemma?"

"The kind that won't let you get that particular vehicle... But there may be other alternatives. Give me a second, I'll be right back." Barry smiled and winked before prancing out of the office.

Once he exited, Na'Tosha gave herself a pep talk. "Bitch, you better do what you gotta do. Ain't no shame in yo' game...You need that big body Benz."

Na'Tosha had her mind made up. She wasn't leaving without that car and was willing to do whatever it took to make sure of it.

Barry stepped back into the office and Na'Tosha pushed him up against the wall, opening her blouse, exposing herself.

Barry's tone of voice quickly changed from calm and professional, to loud and flamboyant. "Oh, my God. Girl, what are you doing? Put those up."

"Well, you were the one talking about other alternatives," said Na'Tosha as she tucked her breasts away.

"I am gay—back door ninja—sword fighter. I was referring to other cars when I said other alternatives. Your credit is terrible. Like the worse I've ever seen. You have delinquent accounts from every department store in America. Why didn't you warn me?"

"Warn you about what... The titties? Shit, I was trying to surprise you."

"No, silly ass. About your credit."

"Ohhh." Na'Tosha shrugged her shoulders. "You never asked."

"Look, Ms. Thang. I'm not finsta play wit' you today. Fix yourself up and follow me... Imma take you over to where we keep the cars that people wit' yo' kind of credit qualify for." Barry led Na'Tosha into an area of old, dusty, and damaged salvage vehicles. "Now, these cars are more up your alley."

"Unnn uhhh. Who finna be driving that?" asked Na'Tosha.

"Well, unless you got another social security number somewhere off in them tig ol' bitties, or one hell of a co-signer, this is all we're going to be able to do for you, boo boo. Make up your mind and let me know what you gon' do. Imma be in the restroom washing my damn eyes out." Barry sashayed down the hall. "I can't believe this skeeza just busted her twins out like that. Un uh, chile... They don't pay me enough for this."

Na'Tosha pulled out her phone and called the only person in the world that she knew with good credit. *"Hey, Mo, girrrll."*

CHAPTER TWENTY-SEVEN

Monique strutted into Tandem Solar Systems with a bright smile and a special twinkle in her eyes. It was a gorgeous afternoon, and Monique's last two scheduled meetings canceled at the last minute. She decided to surprise the love of her life with lunch. Anytime Monique could be in Mario's presence, was a present. The dynamic duo's affection for one another grew with the passing of Ida Mae with Mario's act of compassion shining brightly during Monique's most desperate time of need. In exchange, she gave him the ultimate sign of gratitude by completely letting her guard down. That was a feat that no other man had ever been able to accomplish.

Monique's phone rang as she entered the building and Na'Tosha's name and face flashed across the screen.

"Hey, Mo, girrll... What yo' beautiful, fine, brilliant self doin'?"

"Hey... I'm walking into Mario's job to surprise him with lunch."

"Tell my big homie, Marquis I said, hey. What y'all eatin'?"

"I'll tell Mario you said, hello... Well, I'm bringing him Thai food, but I threw on some of that new Burberry perfume that he bought me sooo... He just might be eating neck and thighs today."

"Okkkayyy. You so nasty."

"Ain't I? But anyways... What do you want? Because I can clearly tell by your tone that you want something."

"Who, me? Daaaang, I can't just call and say, hey?"

"Na'Tosha, stop playing with me."

"Okay, okay, okay... I might, maybe, kind of need an itty-bitty tiny, little favor."

"I should've known."

"I'm at the car lot, and I need a co-signer for this whip I'm trying to buy. Girl, it's shiny, red, with leather interior. I'm talkin' big body bitch. Like, Na'Tosha make the ballas wanna stuurr, big body... Please, boo... Please. I gotta have this car. I'll do whatever you want me to, please."

"Ugh, stop begging."

"Okay, I'll stop... Will you do it?"

Monique initially didn't want to do it. But, after thinking about everything that Na'Tosha had recently gone through, she gave in. *"Yeah, I'll do it. Have them email me the paperwork."*

"Ahhhhhhhhh," Na'Tosha shouted so loud that everyone in the entire dealership took notice.

Monique laughed. *"I'm getting on this elevator. I have to go... Bye."*

As the elevator door opened, everything went into slow motion. She witnessed Mario heavily engaged in a conversation with a mysterious woman. The woman was tall, dark, and lovely. Her perfect smile seemed to make Mario blush. Monique's suspicion grew as the two interacted. It definitely didn't appear to be a regular, work-related, chit-chat. Mario was so wrapped up that he didn't even notice Monique standing there with her arms crossed and mouth poked out.

"Hey, baby... Umm... What are you doing here? I mean... Good to see you... Umm... You look great."

Mario kissed Monique, but her eyes didn't budge from the strange woman's face.

"Uhh, who is this?" asked Monique with an aggressive tone.

Mario nervously responded, "Oh, I'm sorry... Excuse me... Mo, this is Gwen... Gwen, this is my lovely lady, Mo."

"Hi Mo, nice to finally meet you... I've heard so many great things about you." Gwen extended her hand.

Monique glanced at Gwen's extended hand and said, "The name is Monique."

Gwen tilted her head and smiled before stepping out of the elevator. "Hey, Mario... Call you later?"

"Yes, of course... Have a great day... Talk to you later."

Gwen smiled and waved. "Bye."

Monique ice-grilled a hole through the back of her head. Gwen's "bye" had too much extra on it for Monique's liking. The whole encounter came across as sketchy so she gave Mario the "stank" face, and aggressively shoved him his lunch.

"Baby, thanks for lunch. You really know how to take care of your man... It smells delicious," said Mario.

Monique cut right to the chase. "Who is she?"

Mario stuttered. "She's a... A... A colleague... That's all. Strictly business related. You have nothing to worry about. Baby, I promise." Mario kissed Monique on the forehead.

Monique stared into Mario's eyes to let him see that she meant business. "Okay Mario. I'm going to trust you on this one. But don't ever get it misconstrued... I'm only going to say this one time... I'm most definitely not the one to be fucked with. So, think carefully before you ever choose to do so."

Monique was a corporate executive and a well-accomplished woman but was fully capable of acting a fool at the drop of a dime. Especially when it came to something considered to be hers.

Monique's "resting bitch" face caused Mario to panic. She swung her head around just in time to see him staring at the ceiling while forcing down a gulp of his own saliva. The two rode the elevator to Mario's office in total silence.

Lunch was over and the couple sat on the sofa in Mario's office, kissing and holding hands.

Mario and Monique held hands in route to the entrance of the building. "So, we're still on for dinner tonight?" asked Mario.

"Yes, we are... Your place or mine?"

"Let's do mine... We'll switch it up. I'm cooking for you tonight."

Monique did a cute little two step number and raised her hand in the air. "What?"

"Yep... See, I figured I'd run you a nice hot bath, light some candles, feed you an amazing meal, and give you a full body massage."

"Did you say full body?"

"Baby as full as it can get. Then, I'm going to rub your scalp until you fall asleep."

"Can we get started on this now? To hell with the rest of the day."

"To who?"

"Boy, bye. Hell is not a curse word. It is in the Bible."

Mario laughed. "Whatever you say, beautiful... How's eight o'clock sound?"

"Eight o'clock it is."

Mario wrapped his arms around Monique. "I love you."

Monique's heart melted at the sound of Mario's confession. "Aww, baby. I love you more."

CHAPTER TWENTY-EIGHT

Monique soaked in soothing bubbles emerging from the jet streams of Mario's oversized Jacuzzi tub. Ella Mai's hit song, "Trip" played in the background.

Mario tapped on the door twice before entering. "Hey, baby... You doing okay in here?"

"Oh, my God. This bubble bath is everything."

"Perfect. Here's some fresh towels... Dinner will be ready in ten minutes."

Monique sank deeper into the comfort of the warm water. "Baby, why are you so good to me?"

Mario bent down and gave her a kiss. "Because that's exactly what you deserve... Now, let me go take the lasagna out of the oven before I end up barbequing it."

Monique smiled. "Yeah... How about you go do that." Monique exited the tub feeling like a brand-new woman. She dried off and pranced into the bedroom. After putting on her night gown, Monique noticed Mario's phone ringing on top of the dresser. As badly as Monique wanted to answer it, she decided against it. Mario had never given her a reason not to trust him, but the situation from earlier still weighed heavily on Monique's mind. It was something about the way Gwen looked at him that made her uneasy. Mario's suspect behavior inside of the elevator didn't make things any better. The Monique of the past would've spazzed out on both of them. Luckily, she was a woman trying to change. She was tired of carrying the stigma of being the overly independent, angry black woman. With that being said, Mario would receive the benefit of the doubt until proven otherwise.

The couple stretched out on the plush sectional in his living room. Both were feeling full from the meal Mario prepared.

"I'm so stuffed... That was amazing."

"Thank you, my queen. I'm glad you enjoyed it..."

"Who taught you how to make that?"

"It was a family recipe passed down from generation to generation. One thing my mom made sure she did was teach all her boys to cook. That way she knew no matter what, we'd at least be able to feed ourselves."

"That was smart. Thank you, future mother-in-law."

Mario kissed Monique's hand. "Mmmm, you smell so good... I'm going to take a quick shower so we can start on that massage I promised you earlier."

"Yaasss, massage...Yaaasss," said Monique.

"Hold that thought. I'll be right back." Mario rushed towards the bedroom.

Monique searched for the cable remote but instead noticed Mario's phone sitting on the coffee table. Temptation and curiosity increased, as she mentally replayed the elevator scene.

Mario was a great man. Yet, still a man. Monique needed to know if there was more to the situation than an innocent co-working friendship. Ida Mae had always told her that if you searched, you were sure to find. But the thought of being played by who she thought was the man of her dreams, overshadowed Monique's better judgement. Once she heard the shower water running, Monique made her move.

Monique knew Mario's phone was never locked. She often used it to check the time, or make an occasional phone call, but never even thought about going through it until now. It didn't take her long to find what she was looking for. A text thread between Mario and Gwen appeared before her eyes.

Gwen: Hey Mario, how'd you like what I showed you today?
Mario: It was nice, but I'm sure you have a lot more to offer.
Gwen: Of course, I do. My goodies are top of the line.
Mario: I hope so because I'm only interested in the top of the line. I need something that's gonna make my heart skip a beat.
Gwen: LOL I definitely want to get that reaction out of you that's for sure. What is your price range? There are many levels to the services I'm able to provide.
Mario: I don't have a price range. Bring out the best you have to offer.
Gwen: I sure will, but for that we'll need more time and space lol. Can we possibly get together again soon? Preferably somewhere with a darker setting so you can really get the full effect?
Mario: Ritz-Carlton downtown… Can you meet me there tomorrow night @ 9?
Gwen: I'll be there… Bring your wallet you're going to need it lol.
Mario: Great. You just make sure you're ready to show me why you came so highly recommended.
Gwen: I got you, don't worry… Oh, btw… Do you think Monique has any idea? She kind of gave me that

```
impression in the lobby earlier
today.
Mario: Nope. I cleaned it up
smoothly. Mo doesn't have a clue.
Gwen: Perfect. I'll see you tomorrow
night.
Mario: Ok
```

Monique couldn't believe it. Not only was Mario cheating, but he was paying for the services. A feeling of filthiness came over her. Hurt, disgust, and disappointment quickly followed. The flurry of emotion was too much to handle. Monique contemplated grabbing a knife and carving Mario's ass up. She took a few deep breathes. Monique tapped into her brilliant, corporate mind and chose strategy over impulse. She changed back into her clothes and knocked on the bathroom door.

"Hey, Mario?"

"I'm almost done, baby... Three more minutes."

"No, it's okay... My stomach is really bothering me. I think it was all that red sauce from the lasagna. Imma just go home."

Mario turned the shower water off. "Huh? You're going home?"

"Yeah, I'm really not feeling good... Plus, I just realized that I have some last-minute prep work to do for my big presentation in the morning. Sorry, it totally slipped my mind."

"Is it something I can do to help?"

"No, no. I'll be fine... I'm going to get going. I'll text you when I make it home."

Mario quickly dried off with a towel. "Wow... Okay... I hate that you're not feeling well. Let me throw something on real quick so I can at least walk you out to your car."

"Thanks, but there's no need for that. Good night, Mario." Monique moped out of Mario's penthouse suite with the weight of two cinderblocks on her shoulders, while fighting back tears. Her biggest fear had come true. The man she'd given her heart to and let inside of every aspect of her life, turned out to be no different than the rest.

Devastation accompanied Monique on the long ride home. Misery blanketed her as she sulked throughout the night. Sleep was nowhere to be found. The only thing present was the emptiness of her broken heart.

CHAPTER TWENTY-NINE

Monique worked relentlessly the following day. That was a defense mechanism that she'd often used throughout her adult life. Typically, when life dealt her lemons, Monique turned them into a gourmet lemon meringue pie. It was a skillset many admired. Her ability to lock onto a task and block out distractions were second to none. However, this situation was a little different.

Mario's two-timing ways clouded Monique's mind the entire day. She visualized Gwen being the recipient of all the wonderful things Mario had done for her. The thought of his affection being given to another woman caused depression. Did he kiss her on the forehead in the morning? Did he rub her feet and scalp after a long day? Did his smile warm Gwen's heart the way that it had hers? Somehow Monique would have to refocus and block out things that were uncontrollable. She prayed that her fountain of tears would be the first to go.

It was well past 5 p.m., and Monique was still working. She'd been there since 4 a.m. and showed no signs of letting up. She was glued to her laptop when she noticed Rebecca snooping around the door to her office. Although the two didn't have the best relationship, it was apparent that Rebecca was concerned about Monique's energy throughout the day.

"Come in," said Monique as Rebecca softly tapped on the door.

"You're here pretty late... Is everything okay?"

Monique sensed the compassion in Rebecca's voice. "Everything's fine. I'm just getting some prep work done for that big meeting with the Schwartz group."

"I thought that meeting wasn't for another ten days?"

Monique smiled half-heartedly. "You can never start preparing too early, right?"

Rebecca returned the smile. "You're right... Is there anything you need me to do before I take off?"

"Thanks Rebecca, but I'm fine. You go ahead, I'll be here for a while. Have a great weekend."

"Thanks... And same to you."

Monique continued to work but her train of thought was interrupted by the vibrations from her cellphone. She checked the screen and quickly dropped the phone. It was Mario calling for the tenth time. He'd been reaching out since Monique left his place the night before. She wasn't ready to tackle the uncomfortable topic. It was also to Mario's benefit that she took enough time to allow her cooler head to prevail. After ignoring two more of his desperate attempts, Monique decided to listen to what he had to say. But it wouldn't be via conversation. The last of his six voicemails would have to suffice until she was ready to confront him.

> *"Hey baby... I hope that everything's okay. I haven't heard from you since you left my apartment last night, and I'm starting to get worried. Please, call me back or at least text me so I know that you're safe. I love you... Bye."*

Back inside of the office, Monique struggled to concentrate. Gwen's toned legs, nice ass, and adorable smile haunted her. The way she moved, the long good-bye, mixed with Mario's reaction, sent Monique's mind racing. Listening to his smooth-talking voicemail added more botheration to the equation. Her sadness turned into fury.

Monique pounded the desk. "Hell, nah. I'm not going out like that." She closed her laptop and stormed out of the office. There was unfinished business to attend to. The 8 p.m. date at the Ritz-Carlton was going to need a police task-force and a couple of ambulances once Monique was done unleashing the wrath of a woman scorned. It was time to notify the squad.

Eve and Gary cuddled on the couch. The two were on the first episode of what was deemed to be an all-night binge-watching party of the FX hit series, "Snowfall."

"Hello."

"Code blue. Code blue," yelled Monique from the other end of the phone.

"Where."

"My house in an hour."

"Say no more."

"Baby, what's wrong?" asked Gary.

Eve nonchalantly responded. "Oh, nothing... Just a code blue."

"A code blue?"

"Yeah... No biggie." Eve searched through a few drawers inside of the kitchen. "Hey babe, you happened to see any rope or duct tape lying around anywhere?"

Na'Tosha was next to get the emergency call. She was at the nail shop in the middle of a pampering session. *"Hey, Mo."*

Monique's response was short and sweet. *"Code blue my house in an hour."*

Na'Tosha's polish hadn't even finished drying when she jumped up and hustled towards the door. Na'Tosha carefully duck-walked to prevent smearing the dampened paint on her toes. Paying the cashier meant reaching into her purse and potentially ruining her full set. Therefore, Na'Tosha didn't even bother. As she neared the counter, Na'Tosha put on the burners. She raced to the car with the nail tech in hot pursuit.

The tiny Vietnamese lady gave Na'Tosha a run for her money, literally. "You have to pay. You have to pay. Where you go. You have to pay."

CHAPTER THIRTY

The ladies drove down West Olympic Boulevard in route to the Ritz-Carlton. All three were dressed in black like a crew of jewelry thieves on a top-secret heist. Na'Tosha drove, Monique rode shotgun, and Eve occupied the back seat—all three ready to set it off.

"Are you one-hundred percent sure that he's cheating? I mean... What if she really is just a colleague?" asked Eve.

Monique was drained, and her nerves were shot. "I told you I saw the text messages. They're definitely messing around."

"But that doesn't necessarily mean—"

"—Damn bitch, are you scared or something? If she say the nigga cheating, then it's muthafuckin' code blue time. Periodt," said Na'-Tosha.

"Scared? Bitch, I took the blade out my razor, got a full bottle of ninety percent rubbing alcohol to burn a bitch eyes out, and brought the thickest extension cord I could find to tie a muthafucka up with. Hoe, don't play with me," yelled Eve from the backseat.

Monique looked at her GPS. "Hold up... That's the place right there... Hurry up and park."

When the ladies exited the vehicle, Monique was ready for war. Adrenaline rushed throughout her entire body. Her heart pounded intensely and sweat protruded from the palms of her hands. Eve's demeanor was calm as she tightly gripped the extension cord in one hand and the bottle of alcohol in the other. Na'Tosha was turned up to the max, stopping at the entrance of the hotel and cocking her pistol.

"What are you doing? All that might not even be necessary," said Eve.

Na'Tosha smacked her lips. "But just in case it is... A bitch gon' be ready, okkaayy," she said just before tucking it in her waistband.

The ladies bombarded the hotel's lobby. After searching high and low without success, they paraded towards the café.

Monique spotted the two seated at a table near the bar. "There they go right there." She could see Mario holding Gwen's hand. Watching him raise it to the light fired her up even more.

The ladies stormed towards the table. Monique locked eyes with Mario from the moment he caught wind of the stampede storming from his peripheral. She immediately felt the sense of relief in his eyes but also noticed the expression of confusion from the group's unexpected arrival.

"Monique, I've been calling you all day. Wait... How'd you know I'd be here?" asked Mario with great concern.

"No. The question is, what the hell are you doing here with her, Mario?"

"Baby, wait. I can explain..."

"No need to explain. I went through your phone last night and saw y'all little text thread."

Na'Tosha pounded a fist against her palm like a school yard bully, while staring at Gwen. "Just give me the word, Mo. Imma knock her muthafuckin' lights out. Yeah, bitch. I'm talking about you... Ya man-stealing THOT."

Mario tried wrapping his mind around Monique's revelation. "Wait, you did what? Why? I thought you trusted me?"

"Don't try to flip this around. I saw how you both were acting getting off the elevator... Mario, I'm not stupid."

Gwen's face withered with fear as Na'Tosha hovered over her.

"Hey, I'm sorry, Mario but I think I should go."

"Yo' ass ain't goin' nowhere but in the trunk. I wish you would move," said Na'Tosha.

Mario turned towards Gwen. "No, you stay put. I think it's time to go ahead and let her know."

"Right here? Right now?" asked Gwen.

"Yes. Right here... Right now." Mario stared into Monique's eyes. "Monique you're right, I lied... Gwen isn't my colleague."

"You liar. I knew it," cried Monique.

"She's a jeweler," said Mario.

Monique flipped her top. Her vow to stop cursing was null and void. "Fuck you, Mario. I don't give a fuck if this bitch was a muthafuckin' nun. You had no muthafuckin' business..."

"Let me finish, MONIQUE," the bass in Mario's voice thundered throughout the room.

After hearing his roar, each lady gave Mario her undivided attention.

"We've been meeting for the past, couple of weeks... Gwen, hand it to me."

"Which one?" asked Gwen.

"The last one that I looked at... Hand it to me, please."

Gwen handed Mario a five-carat, four-pronged solitaire diamond in a platinum setting engagement ring.

"We've been meeting for the past couple of weeks so I could pick out the perfect engagement ring... For you." Mario dropped to one knee. "Since the day we met, I knew I'd never want to live another day without you. You're the most amazing woman I've ever laid eyes on. Your beauty stretches far and beyond any distance that I could ever travel. Monique Lynnette Harris, you've been the best thing to happen to me in forever, and because of that, I want you to have my last name forever. Although I didn't intend on doing it this way, I don't want to waste another second. Baby... Will you marry me?"

Monique was embarrassed, shocked, and filled with joy. "Yes, baby, yes."

Eve and Na'Tosha teared up in excitement for their sister.

Mario stood and grabbed Monique's hands. The two passionately kissed as Mario held his future wife in his arms. "Now on another note... Monique, if you ever—I mean ever—blatantly disrespect me on some insecure shit like this again, we gon' have some serious problems. Now, do I make myself clear?"

Monique accepted Mario's demand. She had the ring, so submitting to her future king's command wasn't an issue. "Yes, Zaddy."

"All right then, ladies... My fiancée and I obviously have some making up to do. We're going to go ahead and get out of here... Is everyone going to be okay?"

Eve, Na'Tosha, and Gwen all nodded in agreeance.

Mario grabbed Monique's hand. "Okay then. We'll see y'all later... Let's go home, baby... Oh, and thanks once again, Gwen."

"No problem, Mario."

Monique and Mario held hands as they exited the hotel. The past 24 hours had been chaotic for them both. The roller coaster of emotions could've easily ended their promising future. When the smoke finally cleared, Mario proved to be crazy about Monique. Monique just appeared to be crazy. Still in all, true love overshadowed insecurity.

Na'Tosha, Eve, and Gwen were left at the table. Gwen packed her jewelry display to leave.

Na'Tosha gently grabbed her arm before she could take off. "Hey, Gwen, girrll. My bad about all that. I mean... We weren't really gonna throw you in the trunk... Huh, Eve?"

Eve folded her arms and rolled her neck. "Tuh."

"She just playin'... Don't pay her no mind... So, you be havin' all different kinds of jewelry?"

CHAPTER THIRTY-ONE

Eve clumped into her apartment exhausted. Dealing with Monique's shenanigans had really taken its toll. Gary was in the living room doing push-ups. He didn't feel right watching "Snowfall" without Eve, so he opted for a military-styled workout session while he waited on her return.

"Hey, baby... Did everything turn out okay?"

Eve handed Gary the bag of torture items. "Actually, it turned out great. Nobody had to die, and now Monique is engaged."

Gary peeked into the bag and laughed. "I'm not even going to ask."

"Good. Let's just say what started off as a disaster, turned into a happy ending."

Eve seductively slithered towards Gary. She rubbed his sweaty brick wall of a chest.

"You know, I'm all for happy endings," said Gary.

"So am I."

"All right now, woman. Don't start nothing that you're not ready to finish."

Eve grabbed Gary's hand and placed it between her legs. "So, you're telling me that don't feel ready to be finished?"

"What are we waiting for, then?" Gary lifted Eve off of her feet. "Let's get to it."

Eve laughed as she wrapped her legs around Gary's waist. The heat from his tongue electrified her body as they lip-locked their way into the bedroom.

It was 2 a.m., and the two were passed out after wearing each other out. A multitude of hard-thumping bangs at the front door abruptly ended their sweet dreams. The unidentified culprit pounded away like the LAPD serving an arrest warrant. Eve and Gary woke up startled.

"Oh, my God. Who is that?" asked Eve.

"Stay here... Let me go check it out." Gary rolled out of bed and cautiously approached the door. Once there, he glanced through the peep hole.

The loud knocks turned into hard kicks. "Open the muthafuckin' door."

Gary minced back into the bedroom. "It's your ex-husband... And he's drunk. Do you want me to open the door?"

Eve dramatically slammed the back of her head into a stack of pillows piled on her side of the bed. "No. Do not open it."

Deshaun's kicks echoed all throughout the apartment.

"Baby, he's going to' knock the door off the hinges if we don't do something." Gary paced back and forth.

"Why the hell is he here, drunk at two-thirty in the morning?" Eve paused, "And where's my kids?" she jumped out of bed, put her robe on, and scampered out of the room.

"Do you want me to go with you?"

"No, I'll be fine, baby. Just give me a minute." Eve kissed Gary and proceeded to the door.

She opened it and stepped outside. "Deshaun, what the hell are you doing here? It's damn near three o'clock in the morning... Where are my kids?"

Deshaun was so intoxicated that he could barely stand up straight. His words slurred as he talked to Eve. "What you talkin' 'bout, baby? I'm comin' home."

"This is not your home... Where are my kids, Deshaun?"

Deshaun became belligerent. "Bitch, calm down. They're at my momma house. See, that's the reason why I left yo' ass in the first place. Always asking too many questions and shit... Move out the way. I'm tired, I need to lay down." Deshaun tried to push Eve out of the way, but she stood her ground.

"Uhh, no. You won't be lying down in this house... Now, I suggest you go back to wherever you came from before one of my neighbors call the police."

"I'm not worried about the police. Bitch, move out my mutha-fuckin' way." Deshaun pushed Eve again. She did her best to put up a fight, but this time he overpowered her, pushing her to the ground. She laid in agony as Deshaun forced his way inside.

"Stop faking and get yo' ass up. It ain't shit wrong with you." Deshaun made his way into the kitchen. "What you cook tonight? I'm hungry."

Gary appeared from the bedroom, noticing Eve laying in the doorway and Deshaun rummaging through the refrigerator. He hurried to Eve's side, as she cried, and helped her to her feet. All hell broke loose.

Gary darted into the kitchen with blood in his eyes and bad intentions on his mind. He landed a hard-right hook to Deshaun's jaw, dropping him instantly. He brazenly stalked Deshaun's limp body and mounted his chest. Gary pummeled Deshaun's face with repeated Mike Tyson blows. He grimaced with deadly intent as each blow connected.

Blood gushed from every part of Deshaun's face. Immediate swelling formed around his eyes and cheeks. Deshaun's head flopped back and forth as he drifted in and out of consciousness.

Eve desperately pleaded for Gary to stop. Not for Deshaun's sake, but to prevent Gary from killing him and going to jail.

"Gary, stop. That's enough. Please. Baby, stop."

Gary finally came to his senses. After striking one last haymaker, he peeled himself off of Deshaun's mangled body.

Eve dashed into the kitchen and filled a pot with cold water. She poured the entire thing onto Deshaun's face. The shock from the frigid water woke him from his slumber. As Deshaun tried to regroup, Eve back-handed him across his face. "Get out my damn house."

Deshaun mumbled something in an attempt to plead his case.

Eve slapped him again. "Right now."

Deshaun slowly pulled himself up. He held his face and looked towards the bedroom.

Gary stood in the hallway huffing, puffing, and ready for round two.

Deshaun stumbled out of the house. There was no way that he wanted another bout with Gary's hands. The big, bad wolf had met his match.

CHAPTER THIRTY-TWO

Monique and Mario arranged an elegant engagement party at the Ritz-Carlton. The exact place where the lowest point of their relationship reversed into its pinnacle. Family, friends, and colleagues all gathered for this joyous occasion. The Grand Ballroom's forty-foot ceilings, Baccarat Crystal chandeliers, and Versace Mosaic tile floors perfectly set the event's ambience.

Maestro's Steakhouse of Beverly Hills catered the celebration. Tender cuts of Filet Mignon, thick, juicy imported lobster tails, and world-famous garlic mashed potatoes were served to the party goers. Chinook salmon and Swordfish was provided for those who opposed red meat. Rosè champagne and imported, vintage wine filled the participants' glasses.

Smiles and laughter graced the faces of everyone in attendance. The beautiful couple entertained the guest with tremendous hospitality. Monique took a second to admire the scenery. Never in her wildest dreams could she imagine something so perfect. Seeing all her favorite people united in one building was overwhelming. The only person missing was the one who mattered most. Monique smiled as a lonely tear trickled down her cheek. Although Ida Mae wasn't there physically, her unique presence was strongly felt in spirit.

Na'Tosha made her typical "fashionably late" arrival. Immediately, she recognized a common theme of couples in harmony. It didn't take long to realize that she was the exception. The energy in the room made her uncomfortable. Every pair's happiness and affection was a sad reminder of her loneliness. She wanted to pull it together in order to be happy for Monique. But it took a strong individual to support something that was a constant reminder of his or her own short comings. Na'Tosha wasn't quite there yet.

Mario tapped his forks against his glass to garner the room's attention. Both gave compelling speeches expressing their love for one another.

Na'Tosha isolated herself in the distance. Normally, being the oddball didn't bother her. But in this instance, it made her feel like a failure.

The lovely bride-to-be finished addressing the crowd and continued mingling. Na'Tosha momentarily blocked the envy from her heart and approached Monique. The two embraced, but the excitement was definitely one sided.

"Congrats, Mo."

"Thank you sooo much. The closer it gets, the realer it seems. I can't wait to pick out my dress... Oh, and the flowers too."

"That's what's up."

"So far, I know that the color is going to be teal. But, I'm not so sure about the decor yet... So, I was thinking... Maybe you, Eve, and I could get together sometime soon to go over some ideas..."

Na'Tosha glanced into the opposite direction with a stank look on her face.

Monique sensed that something was off about her. "Hey, are you okay?"

Na'Tosha lied, "Not really... I'm not feeling good. I've been cramping all day, and I have a bad headache."

"That's not good... I think I have some Aleve in my purse—let me go check." Monique started towards her purse, before being stopped by Na'Tosha.

"No, it's okay. Imma just head home and lay down. I have a lot of heads to do tomorrow... I probably need to rest anyways. Congratulations once again."

Na'Tosha's excuse sounded similar to Monique's reasoning for leaving Mario's place a while back. Monique knew that something was strange but she was in too good of a mood to dig into it.

Eve and Gary were out on the dancefloor. The frisky couple double-fisted champagne, while bumping and grinding the night away.

When Eve noticed Na'Tosha heading for the exit, she danced over to Monique in order to find out what was going on.

"Heeeyyy, bride-to-be. Where's Na'Tosha going?"

"Home... She said that she wasn't feeling good."

Eve tried to lighten things up. "Well, at least we know her ass ain't pregnant... That's for damn sure."

Monique was still concerned but managed to force a smile after Eve's untimely joke. "That part."

Eve grabbed Monique's hand. "Girl, come on... It's time to go get all that thottin' out of your system before you walk down that aisle."

"The thottin' might stop. But the freakin' with my man is just getting started."

"Cor-rec-tion, ba-byyy. That's not ya man... It's ya fiancé, boo boo. And soon to be husband. No more of that 'my man' talk." Eve lifted Monique's left hand to the light. The five-carat, flawless boulder glistened like a disco ball. "Don't get it twisted. This fat rock on yo' finger says that you're wifey now."

CHAPTER THIRTY-THREE

It'd been a month since Monique's gathering and Na'Tosha was camped out in Eve's parking lot, listening to music. Her despair increased drastically over the past few weeks.

Na'Tosha teetered with the notion of being a supportive sister, and a borderline hater. It wasn't anything personal towards Monique because Monique had been a loyal best friend, always having Na'Tosha's back. However, Monique's celebratory state, coincidentally heightened Na'Tosha's relationship demise. All she ever wanted was to be loved unconditionally. To the point that male or female counterparts didn't matter.

Deep down Na'Tosha was truly happy for Monique. If anyone deserved to live happily ever after, it was her. Na'Tosha leaned on both "Mary Js" to combat the negative vibes. The combination of soul-songstress Mary J. Blige, and the sticky, sweet-smelling aroma of Mary Jane acted as her refuge.

Inside, Eve and Monique laid out color-coordinated patterns of fabric swatches along the dining room table. The beautiful shades of material ranged from vibrant pinks and oranges, to pastel blues and yellows. Monique had her sights set on teal, but Eve's intentions were to change that. Unlike Na'Tosha, she was fully committed to making

Monique's wedding a success. So, doubling as an unofficial, assistant wedding planner was right up Eve's alley.

Eve lost track of time day dreaming of all the ways to make Monique's wedding perfect. The other co-maid of honor was late, as expected, an hour and a half, to be exact. That was overboard even for Na'Tosha's standards.

"Na'Tosha ass is always late." Eve continued organizing the table when she heard what appeared to be music coming from the parking lot. She vaguely heard what sounded like "Not Gon' Cry" by Mary J. Blige. She poked her head out of the window just in time to spot Na'Tosha attempting one of Mary's famous high notes. Eve knew the only time Na'Tosha listened to old school R&B was when something was bothering her.

"What the hell?" uttered Eve on her way down the stairway. She opened the passenger door to NaTosha's new Mercedes and a cloud of ganja smoke greeted her.

Na'Tosha's hideous vocals were right behind. "I was yo' lover and yo' secretary… Workin' every day of the weeeek. Was at the job when no one else was there, HEEELLPPPINN YOUUUU GEETT ONNN YOOO FEEETTT."

Eve took a seat inside. "Girl, what's the matter?"

"I'm good." Na'Tosha turned the music down and wiped her tears as a puff of smoke left her lips.

Eve fanned the weed cloud away from her face. "No, you're not… How long have you been out here?"

"I don't know… I lost track after the fifteenth time I listened to this song."

"Boo, do you want to talk about it?"

Tears rained down as Na'Tosha poured her heart out. "It's just… It's just that here we are together, planning Mo's wedding. She's so happy with Mario, and it seems like they're perfect together. You have Gary who's a great guy. He respects and treats you so well… But I'm out here all alone… Lonely and miserable. I always end up in the same position. Time after time, picking the wrong dudes. Shit, even the wrong females, too." Na'Tosha dropped her head. "Is it something wrong with me? Am I that bad of person to deserve this shit? I want to get married. I want kids. I want a family. This shit just ain't fair."

"Na'Tosha, you're the most beautiful and loyal, ride-or-die friend in the world. You're strong, confident, ambitious, not to mention, talented. I've always admired these things about you. When you step into a room, your presence alone commands every man's undivided attention. Problem is, the men or the women who you've decided to give your attention to, never really deserved it in the first place. Honey, you can't keep expecting different results by taking the same approach. The cars, the clothes, the jewelry. All of that is nice, but none of that stuff means anything if the person behind it doesn't have your best interest at heart. There are plenty of men who'd go over and beyond to give you the world if you just gave them an opportunity. But in order to have that happen, you're going to have to look beyond what he or she has to offer you material-wise. Baby, you have to pay more attention to how they're able to add true, unconditional value to your life. Because in the end, that's what's most important."

Na'Tosha couldn't deny the facts of Eve's statement. "I mean, you're right... But growing up watching my daddy move a certain way in the streets always infatuated me. He spoiled the hell out of me and my momma. All the cars, shoes, clothes, bags, vacations. He always kept us with the nicest things. I knew that's what kind of person I wanted once I got older. But what I didn't realize was all the other stuff me and my momma had to deal with because of it. I'm just so used to a certain lifestyle... I don't know anything different."

"Just imagine how your mom must've felt, knowing that at the drop of a dime, life as you both knew it, could change. To know that the man she gave her life to could be taken away with one false move. That's no way to live, hun."

Na'Tosha dropped her head. "I know."

"Just use this alone period as an opportunity to get yourself together spiritually, mentally, physically, and financially. That way, when God does bless you with a good, hardworking, intelligent, respectful man—or woman," Eve paused to make eye contact with Na'Tosha, "Not a street nigga. I repeat, NOT... A... STREET... NIGGA... That way you'll be fully qualified to not only attract him, but you'll have what it takes to keep him, as well."

Na'Tosha cracked a smile. "Well, my body already snatched. So, that's one less thing I gotta' focus on."

"There you go, boo," said Eve.

Na'Tosha hugged Eve. "Thanks... I really needed this."

"You know I love yo' crazy ass. Now, Mary J... Can we go upstairs and work on this wedding? We're already two hours behind."

"Well, bitch y'all already knew I was gon' be late from jump. Then Mary J ass got to speakin' to me... Had a real one all in her feelings and shit. I'm way too cute fa all dat."

"Girl, bring yo' ass on." Eve laughed as both ladies exited Na'Tosha's red Mercedes.

The heart-to-heart was exactly what Na'Tosha needed. The weight of emotions lifted from her shoulders, and she was free to return to being the solid foundation that Monique rightfully deserved.

"All right, bitch. Let's do it. This wedding finna be bomb. So, we gon' have purple, and teal roses everywhere, but everything else gon' be white. White piano, white seats, white walls, white carpet. I'm doing everybody hair with the best weave not that cheap shit them other hoes be wearing... As a matter of fact, who else gon' be in it wit' us? I hope Mo crusty-ass God sister, Sunshine ain't finna be no bridesmaid. She gon' kill our whole entire vibe..." Na'Tosha rambled as they approached the apartment.

Eve shook her head. "Oh, Lord."

Na'Tosha indeed was back to her old self.

CHAPTER THIRTY-FOUR
Wedding Bells on the Horizon

Monique narrowed her immense variety of wedding dresses down to five. She'd been trying on gowns all month, and the other two ladies were becoming restless.

"Bitch. How 'bout you just say, fuck it, and come down the aisle in a thong and bra?" said no one on earth other than Na'Tosha.

"Mo, please don't mind this heffa. Go ahead and retry on the five you like the most so we can hurry up and get you all the way together."

Monique modeled four of the five. All of them were beautiful, but each was missing something. Fifth dress was the charm. The mother of pearl, mixed-lace, sweetheart neckline, fit and flare gown fit her physique like a glove.

Monique exited the dressing room. "Ladies... How do I look?"

Eve and Na'Tosha marveled at Monique's beauty. After giving each other a look of approval, the two saluted Monique with two thumbs up.

The bachelorette party was next on the calendar. Na'Tosha's opportunity to put her stamp on the wedding events had finally presented itself. She took an unconventional approach to selecting talent for the function. Na'Tosha recruited nine female dancers, and one male stripper. Monique wasn't too fond of male performers, and because they'd always had a ball at gentleman's clubs, the selection of women over men wasn't a huge deal. With that being said, there was one man that every woman's eyes needed to feast on before officially tying the knot. Mandingo Manny was the top male exotic dancer in all of L.A. His skillset easily earned him the Admiral accolade.

The select group of ladies in attendance gathered around the stage. Megan Thee Stallion's "Big Ole Freak" came blasting through the surround sound. Monique was seated in a chair, blind-folded in the middle of the dancefloor. Manny slowly made his way over.

Before he could start his routine, Sunshine, Monique's God sister got a little bit ahead of herself. "That's a whole lot of meat swinging from that tree. Let me g'on 'head and get me some." Sunshine did a cartwheel, combined with a double, back-flip, and landed into Manny's arms.

The ladies in attendance exploded with cheers confusing Sunshine's spectacle as a part of the routine. To their defense, it wasn't every day that a woman her size showed such athleticism. She was considered compact for better terms. Her 5-foot, 300-pound frame wasn't intended to defy laws of gravity.

Manny collapsed onto the floor with Sunshine positioned in reverse cowgirl. She twerked as he wept in excruciating pain. That definitely wasn't the grand finale Na'Tosha had in mind when she planned the event.

The theatrics of the evening left the ladies in tears, laughing their eyes out until the paramedics carted Manny away.

Eve and Na'Tosha waited as Monique talked to the EMT workers.

"Bitch, I'm so hungry, I could eat a lion," said Na'Tosha.

"I think I just spotted one who just might feed your appetite. Looky-looky over there, honey."

Na'Tosha surveyed the room. "Where?"

"Nine o'clock."

"It ain't nine o'clock, bitch, it's two-fifteen in the mornin'. Talkin' 'bout some damn nine o'clock. Girl, yo' ass crazy."

"No, drunk ass. Over there... nine o'clock." Eve pointed in the handsome man's direction.

"Oh, girl he is fine. Wit' his cute, lil' nerd glasses on... And he look like he ain't never been to jail before either. I'm finna go get him."

"Go ahead, then... What are you waiting for? Handle yo' business."

Na'Tosha adjusted her breasts in her dress. "Hoe, watch me work." She trotted over to her target with a sexy strut. As she approached, Sunshine appeared out of nowhere.

Na'Tosha's bottom lip dropped and she slammed her hands against her thighs as Sunshine amazingly repeated her patented flip routine onto the unidentified man. Only this time the man caught her, and impressively kept his balance. The two made out in a sloppy, grotesque way as the gentleman struggled to keep from falling. Come to find out, the guy was Sunshine's new man, Danny.

Na'Tosha back-pedaled towards Eve. "Can you believe this shit? Even Sunshine got somebody—and a fine one at that."

Both stared in disgust as Sunshine and Danny practically ate each other's faces off.

"There went my appetite," said Eve.

Na'Tosha's stomach growled. "Oh, well... If it wasn't meant to be, it wasn't meant fa me. Let's go get somethin' to eat."

"You still hungry after that?"

"Bitch, please, I'm starvin'... Go get Mo ass so we can go. That taco truck on Pico callin' my name as we speak, okaaay."

THE BIG DAY

"Mo, sweetie, you have to hurry up. I know you're nervous and all but damn. You on Na'Tosha time now," said Eve after fending off the wedding planner for the third time.

"Ummm, sis, don't do me... I'm here ain't I? Shit, if she gettin' cold feet, give me the ring, and let me put the dress on," said. Na'Tosha.

Eve galloped towards her. "You know what..."

The two bickered for several minutes like two nine-year-olds.

At last, Monique emerged from the bathroom in glamorous form with her face beat by makeup artist extraordinaire, D'ara Denise, and her perfectly contoured face to mirror her smooth, caramel-brown skin tone. A pair of Cartier earrings matched the diamond-encrusted headpiece that wrapped around her forehead like the crown of a Nubian queen. Monique's sheer veil elegantly draped down to the Cathedral train of the off-white, form-fitted wedding gown. Christian Louboutin's "Degrastrass" heels, sealed the deal.

Eve and Na'Tosha gasped in astonishment.

"You look so amazing," said Eve.

Na'Tosha fanned herself. "Oh, my God. Bitch, I'm finna cry."

"You can't use bitch and God in the same sentence." Eve put her hand on her hip.

"But you just did tho'... Ha." Na'Tosha childishly licked her tongue out.

Monique interrupted the quarrel with words she'd been waiting to say her entire life. "Okay... I'm ready."

The church was packed from wall to wall. Case's "Happily Ever After" set the mood for the bride's coveted walk down the aisle. Monique gallantly ambulated along Denisha's rose pedaled pathway with the grace of a Royal Highness. She couldn't help but smile as she observed the strong, dominant, brave groom-to-be withering at the sight of her stunning beauty. At that moment it all set in. Soon she'd be joined in Holy matrimony to her knight in shining armor.

Once at the altar, she looked towards the Heavens above, where an image of Ida Mae formed into the ceiling. Next to her were silhouettes of her late mother and father. Monique smiled with tears of joy in her eyes. She knew that her three guardian angels were staring down, prouder than ever.

Eve's heart warmed as she watched her best friend dazzle the crowd. The most ambitious, determined, supportive person she'd ever encountered, finally found someone who was worthy of her love. She couldn't have been any happier for Monique. Eve looked into the audience to locate the man who helped restore happiness back into her own life. There, Gary was handsome as ever. Eve was in love again and was getting excited about a possible future marriage for herself. But that would be later down the line. Until then, the two would enjoy the journey of learning one another more each day.

Eve waved to her man, and Gary returned it with one of his own.

Na'Tosha blew a kiss in the same direction.

"What's wrong with you? Don't be blowing kisses at my man!" said Eve to Na'Tosha as they took their places along the steps of the altar.

"Yo', man? Trick, I brought my own plus-one."

Seated directly behind Gary was Na'Tosha's guest, Chaz, the Footlocker-slash-Uber-slash-Lyft driver that she kept bumping heads with. Eve's talk about stepping outside of the norm to find better results, reminded Na'Tosha of the cute guy who she'd given a hard time.

Chaz Dawkins was a former collegiate athlete from the Bay Area. He was a light skinned, baby-faced man in his late twenties. Chaz stood 6'5" with chiseled arms and abs of steel. He was a former basketball prodigy destined for the NBA. Sadly, injuries prematurely put an end to his dreams of making it big. Chaz remained in the Los Angeles area after losing his hoop scholarship at the University of Southern California. He was determined to fulfill two promises he made to his late mother. First, to obtain his degree by any means necessary. The second promise was to never return to Oakland without making something of himself. Chaz took online classes and worked two jobs to make ends meet.

Na'Tosha humbly forced herself back to the mall to right her wrongs. Once there, she spotted Chaz returning from lunch with a Chick-fil-A bag and lemonade in his hand.

"Can I have some?" said Na'Tosha with a sly grin.

Chaz halted and turned around to the sound of her distinct ratchet voice.

"Ah, it's you again? Listen, I'm not really in the mood for yo' bull-shit today."

"Dammnn, now you're the one not in the mood, huh? Calm down Mr. One Star. I didn't come here for all that?"

Chaz sipped from his lemonade while giving Na'Tosha an apprehensive look.

"Well, I'm not on the clock for another five-minutes, but I'm sure there's a few guys in there who wouldn't mind helping you out." As Chaz made his way towards the store's entrance, Na'Tosha said something that totally threw him off guard.

"I don't want their help—I want yours."

Chaz hiked his eyebrows in disbelief before slowly approaching Na'Tosha. "What do you mean, you want my help? What can this 'shoe salesman-Uber-slash-Lyft-driver' do for you besides 'stop counseling and start driving?' That is what you told me to do, right?"

As he got closer, Na'Tosha dropped her head and fidgeted her thumbs.

"I mean what possibly can a plain ole, regular, barely getting by dude like me do for a spoiled, uppity diva like you?"

Na'Tosha slowly raised her head and peered into Chaz's eyes. The two were now so close that she could smell the Jean Paul Gautier cologne rising from his chest. "You can start by taking me out to eat. We can figure all the rest out later."

Chaz laughed at her audacity. "Wait, is that your way of apologizing? By telling me that I can take you out to dinner? Ha. Yeah, okay."

Na'Tosha grabbed his arm before he could turn away. "Okay, okay. Look, lately I've been doing some soul searching, and I realize my mouth can be a little too much at times..."

"A little?"

"Yeah, nigga a little—you heard what the fuck I said."

The corners of Chaz's perfect lips turned downward.

"My bad. I'm a work in progress don't judge me—I guess what I'm trying to say is..." Na'Tosha dropped her head again before mumbling. "I'm sorry."

"What was that? Come again." Chaz raised his hand to his ear. "I couldn't hear you."

Na'Tosha mumbled again, "I'm sorry."

"A little louder please, I still couldn't make out what you said."

"You know what? Fuck it. Nevermind." Na'Tosha stomped off with her heels blazing the floor.

Chaz quickly trotted behind her. "Hey, lighten up. I was just playin' wit' you."

"Do I look like the one to be playin' wit'? The fuck."

Chaz flashed his pearly white grin. "Nah—you look like the one Imma be taking to dinner Saturday night. Here, take my number down."

Na'Tosha blushed as she pulled out her cellphone. "Is that right?"

Chaz licked his lips. "Absolutely."

And from there, the rest was history.

Was Chaz a baller? No, but he was a hard-working, God-fearing man, with two jobs and a plan. That was a huge difference in what Na'Tosha was used to, but also a great step in the right direction.

Chaz caught the air-kiss that Eve thought was intended for Gary. He provocatively put it inside of his pants and blew Na'Tosha one back.

She snatched Chaz's kiss out of the air and put it underneath her dress. The two definitely matched each other's nastiness.

"Eeeooowwww," said Na'Tosha in Cardi B's voice.

Eve covered her face. “Oh, Lord.”

• • •

Everyone from young to old, sang, danced, ate, and drank at the reception. The newly Mr. and Mrs. Ferguson couldn’t have asked for a better turn out. The genuine support from loved ones magnified an already monumental day.

When it was time for the highly anticipated bouquet toss, all the single ladies, aspiring brides, and women in between, lined up onto the dancefloor. Eve and Na’Tosha didn’t see any other competition outside of themselves.

“Don’t get in my way. I'm tellin’ you now, Imma run yo’ ass over,” said Na’Tosha.

Eve didn’t back down. “Don’t play, this my bouquet. You know I use to hoop a lil’ bit back in the day. I still got hops.”

Na’Tosha cracked her knuckles. “Hoop? Boo boo, this a real contact sport right here, okaaay. If you’re not ready to get down and dirty, go sit yo’ ass down.”

Monique’s shrewd receptionist Rebecca intervened. “Ladies, it’s not that serious... Let’s all calm down and have some class about ourselves.”

Eve and Na’Tosha glanced at one another. Miss “stick up her ass” obviously didn’t know that she was messing with the wrong ones.

“Bitch, shut up,” screamed both ladies as they took position.

Rebecca stormed off in a fit of rage as the ladies mocked her brat-like hissy fit.

The bride was ready to make the toss. “Okay ladies... Ready... One... Two... Three.”

In slow motion, the bouquet of flowers flew into the ladies’ direction. Eve and Na’Tosha boxed each other out like two basketball players fighting for a rebound. Na’Tosha, in a desperate effort, tripped Eve onto the ground. The bouquet was almost in her grasp. As she reached out to snag the coveted prize, an unexpected contender threw a wrench into Na’Tosha’s program.

Acrobatic, swift-footed, twist master Sunshine, leaped into the equation with accurate precision. She flipped and tumbled before snatching the bouquet from Na’Tosha’s finger tips.

"I caught it. I caught it. Look, bae. I caught it." Sunshine sprinted over to her man, Danny. She tackled him to the ground, and the two swapped spit like Grizzly bears in heat.

Na'Tosha had been duped by Sunshine once again. She balled her fist, bit her bottom lip, and stumped towards the victor's direction. She cocked her arm back with the intention of knocking Sunshine into next week before Monique reached out and grabbed her arm.

"Let me find out you're being a sore a loser," said Monique with a giggle.

Na'Tosha turned to Monique and exhaled. "I'm gettin' real sick and tired of her ass."

"AHEM—AHEM" grunted Eve as she sat on the floor trying to get the ladies' attention, "So, y'all just go'n leave me on the damn floor, huh?"

Monique and Na'Tosha raced over to help Eve, but once they reached their arms out, she yanked both ladies to the ground alongside of her. The two thumped onto the ballroom floor, landing awkwardly.

"Ouch—bitch, that hurt," said Na'tosha, before popping Eve on the arm.

Eve chuckled. "That's what yo' ass get for pushing me down here."

"Well, what the hell did I do?" said the bride while rubbing her elbow.

Eve and Na'Tosha both stared at Monique before echoing one another. "I thought you wasn't cussin' no more?"

Monique scrunched her face and paused. "Hell isn't a curse word—"

The other two ladies rolled their eyes and finished her sentence for her. "Yeah, yeah—we know—it's in the Bible."

"Shut up!" yelled Monique as she lunged at them both. The three piled on top of each other, laughing happily like they'd done as kids.

TO BE CONTINUED...

All I Do Is Pen Publishing Presents

Deshaun's Road to Redemption: A Black Man's Battle With Mental Illness
By C.W. Burnett

From the outside looking in, Deshaun Nelson is a 32 year-old black man plagued with drug addiction, bad attitude, lack of accountability, and extreme anger issues. But beyond the surface lies a much deeper problem. A problem that black men in America have hid from for decades.... MENTAL ILLNESS. After being humbled to his lowest point, Deshaun finds himself in a situation that could land him years behind bars. His only chance of leniency comes in the form of a black, court-appointed therapist, Dr. Julissa Bishop. As Dr. Bishop unravels layers of his murky past, Deshaun is forced to trace the origins of his trauma head on.

www.allidoispen.com
Instagram: all_i_do_is_pen • Facebook: C.W. Burnett

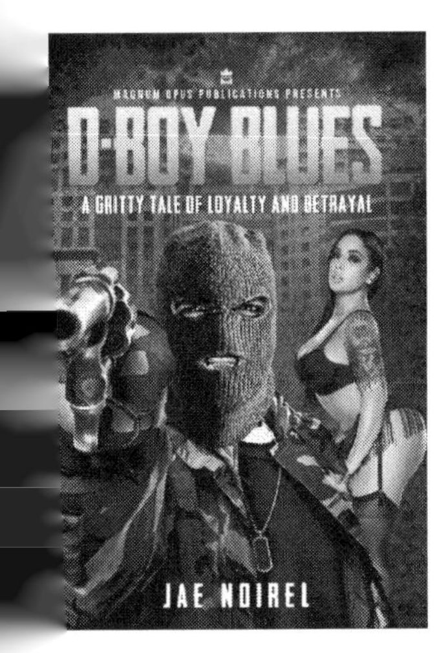

Magnum Opus Publications Presents

D-Boy Blues:
A Gritty Tale of Loyalty and Betrayal
By Jae Noirel

Blue and Bobby grew up together as best friends. Blue is a street smart Hustler being raised in foster care and Bobby is a scrawny nerd who lives with his sister and abusive father. As kids, Blue protects Bobby from neighborhood bullies but as they grow older they grow apart. Bobby grows up to be an Oakland police officer and Blue becomes a prominent drug dealer. This nlikely pair are put at odds once they cross paths in the street and both ve and loyalties will be tested. D-Boy Blues is a classic story of love, etrayal, redemption and police corruption.

www.MagnumOpusPublications.com
Instagram: mgnm_opus • Facebook: Magnum Opus Publications

Made in the USA
Middletown, DE
17 September 2023

38670180R00106